HAPPY HOMICIDE

A FRENCH QUARTER MYSTERY

JEN PITTS

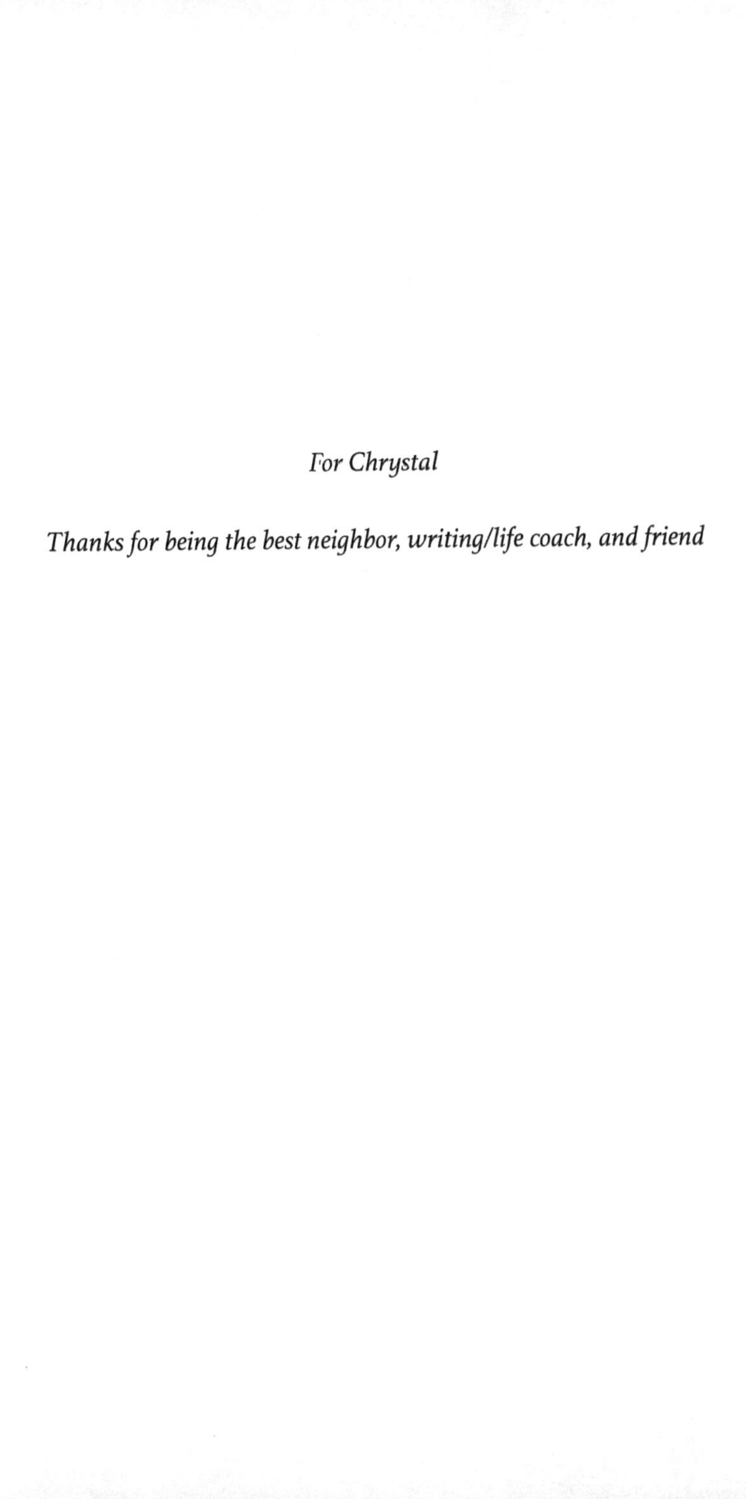

For Chrystal

Thanks for being the best neighbor, writing/life coach, and friend

CONTENTS

1

———

Even with a chill in the air, Momo McBride's balcony was the most relaxing place to be on this early November evening. The light from the candelabra on the iron table cast a soft glow as we sat and sipped our drinks. Although bourbon wasn't my preferred drink, it was Momo's favorite. She always offered it, along with cheese straws, when I came over to visit. Bourbon warmed my body while Momo's chatter warmed my heart. Since I met her seven months ago, her stories made me laugh or cry, and sometimes both.

Tonight we were cackling over her neighbor Gideon's newest addition to his art collection. He lived a few doors down, and Momo had a bird's-eye view of his comings and goings. Earlier today, two men tried and failed to deliver a sculpture.

"Sammy, I don't claim to be an art critic, but no one in their right mind would want that thing for their house." Momo brushed a few loose gray hairs off her wrinkled face. "Imagine an oversized metal rowboat with oars welded to the sides. Then add railroad spikes jutting out willy-nilly, and there you go."

"Railroad spikes? Those must have made it hard to handle."

"Oh, it was. That monstrosity wasn't going anywhere." Momo gestured toward Gideon's town house with her hand that held a cigarette. The ash appeared seconds away from falling onto the already scarred floorboards of the balcony.

"Gideon doesn't like to be told no." I laughed. He frequently invited me to see his art collection, but I always declined. I wasn't worried about my safety, just worried that I'd never get out of there since Gideon loved to hear himself speak. Despite his boastful and flirtatious nature, his philanthropy work made him a bit more tolerable.

"He insisted it'd fit through the front door. That man may be rich, but he isn't spatial one bit."

"Spatial?" I asked.

"Yes, spatial, not special. Although he's not that either." Momo laughed. "My momma used to say anyone who packed a grocery sack with everything fitting just right was spatial. I have that gift. You should see me pack a suitcase for a two-week trip."

"Well, I'm afraid I'm not spatial," I said. "I've been known to leave a hair dryer at the baggage check-in counter."

"But I bet you've never left a book behind."

"Tru dat." I grinned.

"Speaking of books, I have something for you."

"You didn't need to do that, Momo." With my birthday coming up in a few days, friends were giving me gifts if they couldn't make my birthday party. I appreciated all the kind gestures, but it overwhelmed me. I had never had such a large group of friends like I had here in New Orleans.

"Of course I do! While age is merely a number, I feel it's important to acknowledge and celebrate the joys of the past year. And we can drink off the sorrows." Momo lifted her glass, and I clinked mine against hers. This past year I lost my adopted parents, moved from San Francisco to New Orleans, discovered my birth family, and found my new home in the French Quarter. Fortunately, the joys outweighed the sorrows, but they didn't completely erase them from my heart.

"I hope I didn't ruin the surprise for you," Momo said.

"The shape gave it away, not you." I laughed as I accepted the rectangular-shaped package from her.

"You'll have to forgive my use of yesterday's newspaper and kitchen twine for wrapping your gift. I could have sworn I had wrapping paper, but it apparently disappeared."

The comic section brought color to the package since the twine was white. It seemed out of place for Momo, who did everything with her own quirky style. Even her ashtray was a china teacup. Not that I cared how she wrapped a gift. The fact she had a gift for me was more than enough.

I untied the twine, and as it dangled from my fingers, Lady Clementine batted at it. Momo's Siamese cat was very particular about who she interacted with, so I considered it an honor to play with her. She grasped it with her teeth and pulled it back onto the ground. She flopped down with her front paws on the twine and promptly fell asleep.

"Like I said, I knew you would love this. I just couldn't wait until your party," she said.

"Wow, this is amazing!"

Momo gifted me a US first edition copy of Agatha Christie's *Sleeping Murder*. I lightly touched the plain cover, which simply displayed the author's name, book title, and that it was Miss Marple's final case. The book opened stiffly.

This edition was published in September 1976, and I wondered if it had been read much, if at all.

"How did you know I've been looking for this book?"

"I have my ways." Momo's croaky laughter woke up Lady Clementine. The cat meowed and lowered her head back down on the ground. "Oh, sweet kitty, you're all out of sorts with all the comings and goings here."

"What's going on?" My stomach dropped as my imagination ran wild. Was she moving? Did she have financial problems? Then again, perhaps she had good news to share.

"Oh, goodness, I didn't mean to make you worry." Momo squeezed my hand gently. "My old friend, Nora Winslow, moved in last week."

"That explains the murmurs I heard from your guest room. I thought maybe you had found a replacement for Judy," I said.

"I wish. Finding a new housekeeper is proving harder than nailing jelly to a wall. Judy is one of a kind." Momo sighed. "I've stopped looking for now so I can concentrate on helping Nora. When she isn't sleeping, she's reading. Her illness has taken a toll on her body, but not her mind."

Momo explained that Nora Winslow moved in with her last week. They became friends back in 1975 when Nora rented a room from her. Nora moved away, but they stayed in touch. She kept her cancer diagnosis to herself and returned to New Orleans. Once Momo found out, she insisted Nora stay with her. Unfortunately, her medical treatments hadn't provided a cure, so she stopped them and wanted to let nature take its course. Momo couldn't bear the thought of her dying in a sterile hospital room, so she moved her into her guest room on the first floor.

"Nora has few visitors, but tonight her old friends, Lydia Townsend and Dorothy Merritt are here. They've come by all week. I hired Lydia's daughter, Paige, to take care of Nora."

"That was very kind of you, Momo."

"Pshaw, it was nothing. Nora doesn't really need a registered nurse, but Paige is in between jobs, so it was a win-win situation for all of us."

"Well, that explains all the hustle and bustle that is disturbing, Lady Clementine." I reached down and scratched her on her head. She purred but didn't open her eyes.

"Actually, I bought your gift from Nora. She insisted on selling her belongings to help pay for her care. I told her she didn't need to, but she's as pigheaded in her sixties as she was in her twenties." Momo shook her head. "Andrew bought the entire box except your book. He told me it'd make a great birthday present for you, so I bought it from her myself."

Being the co-owner of Lagniappe Books with Andrew Ballard had its benefits, including having access to books from a variety of sources. We purchased new books, but some of our inventory came from estate sales. I'd been looking for this copy of *Sleeping Murder* ever since I became business partners with Andrew in the spring.

"Too bad it's not a signed copy," Momo said.

"It would be a fake if it were. This was published after Agatha Christie died. This was her last book, not just Miss Marple's last case." I turned the pages slowly and stopped when I discovered a pink greeting card-sized envelope. Nora's name was scrawled on the front. "Momo, there's a card addressed to Nora in here."

Momo took the card from my hand and flipped it over. "It's sealed, so I imagine she didn't read it."

"It must have been important since she placed it in the book. I wonder why she didn't open it," I said.

"Let's go find out. This is a mystery for you to solve."

I followed Momo down the stairs to a guest room on the first floor. She knocked and waited until a voice said, "Come in!"

We entered the bedroom to an audience of four women. The two women who had to be sisters by their identical slim noses and distinctive cowlicks, although one had gray hair and the other suspiciously black hair. They sat in two armchairs close to the side of the four-poster bed.

The other woman was decades younger but had the same features as the other women except for her brown hair. She stood on the other side of the room.

Nora Winslow sat up in her bed with three pillows propping up her back. She had a soft-yellow blanket covering her legs, and her hands were folded on the edge of the blanket. Her auburn hair was gray at the roots and hung an inch past her shoulders. Her face was gaunt, but her blue eyes sparkled as she looked at me.

"Hello, there! You must be Samantha Richardson." Nora winced as she stretched out her hand toward me. "Momo has told me all about you. If Momo and Lady Clementine like you, then I will like you."

I grasped her ringless hand gently. "It's a pleasure to meet you, Ms. Winslow. I'm glad Momo and Lady Clementine have vouched for me."

"She's always been a good judge of character. Except when it came to me." Nora's laugh turned into a cough. The younger woman poured a glass of water from a pitcher on the doily-covered nightstand. Nora took a long sip and cleared her throat. "Thank you, Paige."

"Of course, Nora." Paige patted Nora's hand. "Shall I leave you with your company now?"

"We should leave, too," the dark-haired sister said. "Let's go, Lydia."

"Don't leave on our account, Dorothy," Momo said. "We just came down here to give Nora an envelope we discovered in an old book of hers."

"You mean, Samantha's book. It's hers now." Nora smiled at me. "But I assume my name is on that envelope in Momo's hand."

Momo handed the card to Nora, and the smile on her face faded. With shaking hands, she flipped the envelope open and ripped the sealed envelope. Leaning over, I saw hand-drawn holly leaves on the front of the card. Hannah gasped as her sister grabbed her hand. Nora opened the card and ran her finger over the cursive handwriting inside. She closed it before I could read the words, and then she put the card inside the envelope and held it against her heaving chest as she squeezed her eyes shut.

"I knew I shouldn't have killed him."

2

———

There was a stunned silence, and it felt as if the air had been sucked out of the room. Having just met Nora, I had to say that was the last thing I imagined her saying. Even her friends were shocked.

"Nora, what are you talking about? Hollis's death was an accident." Dorothy leaned over the bed and put her hand on Nora's arm. "We've talked about this. You did nothing wrong that night. We know you didn't cause Hollis to fall."

Lydia nodded as her sister spoke, but she bit her lip, as she was keeping herself from speaking. Momo regained her composure and whispered in Paige's ear. They exchanged a few more whispers, then Paige pulled the blanket up on Nora who hadn't opened her eyes or even twitched.

"Mom, Aunt Dorothy, we should let Nora rest." Paige pointed to the door. "You can visit with her tomorrow if she's up to it."

"But we need to know what Hollis said in the card," Lydia pleaded.

"Nora will tell us when she's ready. Or perhaps we can just read the card ourselves. Would that be all right, Nora?"

Dorothy stood up and reached toward Nora's hands. Momo stopped Dorothy by putting her arm in between Dorothy and Momo. Neither said a word to each other, but both had sour faces as they stepped back.

Nora opened her eyes and stared at the ceiling. "Oh, it's nothing important in the card. Can you all excuse me? My medication is making me sleepy." Nora put the card back inside the envelope and handed it to Paige. "Dear, can you put this in the drawer? I need to rest now."

"Of course, Miss Nora." Paige placed the envelope in the top drawer much to the disappointment of Momo and the sisters by the looks on their faces. I couldn't deny I was disappointed, too. But by Nora's reaction, the card shocked her even if she denied it wasn't important. But she wasn't going to speak any more about it right now.

"Get some rest, Nora." Momo placed her hand on Nora's cheek and wiped a single tear that had trickled down her face. "Let's go, everyone."

I opened the door and stepped into the hallway. Dorothy and Lydia didn't acknowledge me as they hurried to the front door. Momo followed them outside, leaving the door open. Her back was toward me, but from Dorothy's and Lydia's dour expressions, Momo wasn't saying anything they wanted to hear.

I turned my attention to Nora. Paige leaned over her patient, nodding slowly as Nora whispered to her. My curiosity got the better of me and I stepped closer to the doorway. The floorboards creaked under my feet so I couldn't eavesdrop. Paige whipped her head around but her irritation turned to relief. Apparently I wasn't a problem for Paige.

"I'm sorry. I didn't mean to interrupt you, Paige. Momo is speaking with your mom and aunt, so I thought I'd see if you needed anything," I rambled, hoping I didn't sound like I was covering up my eavesdropping. Even though I was. Either Nora didn't notice or care.

"You're fine. Nora is going to rest, and it's my time to leave." Paige turned to her patient. "I'm off tomorrow, but you can call me if you need anything or want to talk."

"Thank you, my dear. We'll talk later." Nora smiled at Paige and then me. "Oh, Samantha, you're still here. I'm so sorry we couldn't chat longer. I hope we'll have a chance later on."

"I'd love that. Get a good night's rest," I said.

Paige closed the door behind her and took a brown coat off the standing coatrack in the hallway. "You're a friend of Momo's, right? Are you the one who solved her grandniece's murder?"

"Well, I helped, but I wouldn't say I solved it." My friends said I did solve it, but I had to give credit to Detectives Rob Armstrong and Christine Gammon of the New Orleans Police Department (NOPD). Especially if I didn't want to get in trouble for sticking my nose into places I wasn't supposed to. But my curiosity gets the better of me when a friend needs help.

"That's not what Miss Momo says. Nora might need your help, but not tonight," Paige said.

"Did you believe her when she said she shouldn't have killed your uncle?"

"No, I don't." Paige put on her coat on over her navy-blue scrubs and tied its belt. "But something about that night is bothering her. I don't want her to pass on without having that weight of Hollis's death off her shoulders."

"Not to be disrespectful, but how long does Nora have?" After I said it, I wish I could have taken it back. It wasn't any of my business.

"It could be weeks or months. Tonight's outburst isn't helping her health by any means."

"She did seem exhausted. Is that from her painkillers?"

Paige shook her head. "No, it takes longer for them to kick in. I believe she knew what she was saying."

I shouldn't have been surprised, but I did hope it was just the rambling of a woman on painkillers. But Nora's reaction to the card and her quick sleepiness had me suspicious. Her friends' reactions were unexpected. They didn't just tell her she was being ridiculous; Dorothy said they had already talked to her about Hollis's death.

Before I could ask Paige more questions, Momo came inside and slammed the door shut.

"Your mother and your aunt are the most tiring women sometimes," Momo grumbled as she joined us.

"Welcome to my world, Miss Momo." Paige laughed half-heartedly. "Let me guess: they wanted you to take the card out while Miss Nora is sleeping."

"Bingo. Thank you for standing up for Nora. I realize it must be difficult to stay true to your work ethic when you have those two pestering you," Momo said.

"It's not hard. It's just annoying. My patients come first." Paige walked to the door. Momo followed her, so I did the same. "I'm off tomorrow, but you know to call me if you need me. And I'll keep my family away until Nora wants to speak to them. My uncle's card was for Nora, not them."

"That's true, but I know how much Lydia and Dorothy loved their brother. I remember how devastated they were when he passed away," Momo said.

"They still are."

With that, Paige hurried down the stairs and turned left. As she approached Hotel Jeanne, a stocky man in a vintage blue-and-white varsity jacket rushed out of the hotel's door.

She shook her head as the man approached her but didn't stop him from walking next to her.

"That's Paige's off and on boyfriend," Momo said.

"Is she okay with him?" While the man didn't appear physically threatening to Paige, she didn't seem happy to see him.

"Oh, yes. I asked her the first time he was waiting for her. She said they're still friends." Momo walked back into the house. "Shall we finish our drinks? I'll tell you about Hollis Davenport."

"Lead the way."

3

———

"You ran a boardinghouse?" I pulled the yellow cashmere throw blanket tighter around my shoulders. In the half hour we spent downstairs, the temperature dropped at least ten degrees. Despite the chilly weather, it was worth sitting on the balcony. I'd be willing to sit in an igloo to listen to Momo's story.

"A boardinghouse of sorts. Nora jokingly referred to my house as the home for wayward women."

"By the look on your face, I'd say you enjoyed having students live here." I welcomed Lady Clementine onto my lap and slowly scratched behind her ears.

"Oh, I did. I only took in women students from Sophie Newcomb College. It's my alma mater. Nora was my first. I needed a distraction after my husband died."

Momo had a husband. She never mentioned one, so I wrongly assumed she had always been unmarried. "I'm sorry about your husband, Momo," I said.

"Thank you, darling." Momo's eyes teared up, but she didn't cry. "You must have questions about him, but that's for another day. It's a long story, and right now, we need to concentrate on Nora's past."

I couldn't decide if Momo's tension was from the mention of her husband or Nora's situation. I respected her wishes, but I wanted to hear about her husband. Instead, she continued on with Nora's story.

"Nora considered herself an independent woman and refused to live in a dormitory. Her parents allowed her to live off campus if she stayed in a women's-only boarding-house." Momo laughed. "In the fall of 1975, I opened my door to this tall, lanky woman with a smile as bright as her tie-dye shirt."

Of all of Momo's boarders, Nora quickly became Momo's favorite. She was a thoughtful renter, helping around the house without obligation. Nora helped other boarders with their homework. Momo always knew when Nora had a test, since the scent of a baked apple pie would waft out from the kitchen.

"Her way of studying was to rattle off the material while she cooked. I never had another renter do that before or after."

"How many other boarders did you have?" I asked.

"Oh, I lost count. Some stayed for a semester, some for a few years. I stopped taking in boarders about 1980, so I could travel. When I returned to New Orleans, I decided I'd like some peace and quiet. Of course, that changed when Nicole moved in with me." Momo's voice cracked when she said her grandniece's name.

Nicole's disappearance took a toll on Momo. The discovery of Nicole's body and the truth of what happened to her had helped, but Momo couldn't hide the anguish of losing her grandniece.

Lady Clementine awoke from her nap and stretched out

a paw toward her human. Momo held Lady Clementine's paw for a moment. "I'm all right, little girl. You go back to your beauty sleep."

The Siamese cat did just that. "Nubi does the same thing to me when he thinks I'm sad."

"Cats are amazing creatures." Momo cleared her throat. "Let me get back to Nora. Just a few weeks after she moved in, she told me about a boy she met. I'll never forget the day Nora brought Hollis over to meet me. They were clearly infatuated with each other," Momo said.

"From Dorothy and Lydia's friendship with Nora, I'd say they were happy about the relationship," I said.

"Yes, at first. Nora not only found a boyfriend but also made two new friends. Despite being a few years older, and both being married with children, the three women got on like a house on fire."

"What changed?" I took a sip of my cold bourbon.

"Actually, I believe it was Hollis that changed. As it's with most, if not all, Southern families, the eldest son takes over the family business. Hollis's great-grandfather started Davenport Oil, and it had passed down the line. Hollis's father expected him to take over the family business sooner rather than later."

"Was Hollis much older than Nora? I assume Nora was eighteen if she was just starting college."

"He was twenty-one, and Nora was eighteen when they met. After college, he would run Davenport Oil along with father while his wife would take over the household from Hollis's mother," Momo said.

"And once he met Nora, Hollis made other plans."

Momo took a cheese straw from her plate and pointed it at me. "You are one smart cookie. As the baby of the family, Hollis's mother insisted he have time to sow his oats, so to speak. But they weren't happy when Hollis said he wouldn't take over the family business.

"Hollis fell in love with Nora and her future plans. Nora came to New Orleans planning to graduate with a degree in education and join the peace corps. Six months after they started dating, he decided to finish his degree, and when Nora graduated, they'd join the peace corps together."

"Oh."

"Oh, indeed." Momo shook her head. "As you've guessed, Mr. And Mrs. Davenport were angry. They accused Nora of seducing their son and taking him away from his family. Which wasn't far from the truth. Nora showed him a world outside his family and New Orleans.

"Hollis fought with his parents, naturally. His sisters took a different approach and talked with Nora. They tried to persuade her that staying in New Orleans was what she really wanted. And it would be the best thing for Hollis and her."

"Wow, Hollis was under a lot of pressure from his family. And Nora, too, from the sounds of it," I said. "Since Nora was only a freshman, they had four years before dealing with this issue. If they were even still dating." It seemed like a lot of worrying about something that wouldn't be an issue for a while, if ever.

"Nora moved up her timeline. In September 1976, she decided she wanted to leave school after the fall semester and join the peace corps."

"Let me guess: Hollis decided to go with her," I said.

"Actually, he didn't. He and Nora argued about her plans for almost a month leading up to her birthday. Hollis wanted her to wait until he finished college." Momo shook her head. "She refused, naturally. Nora's independence and confidence made her seem older than nineteen. But her persistence could be that of a child wanting dessert before dinner.

"On her birthday morning, Nora came to the kitchen with a spring in her step.

"'Oh, Miss Momo,'she said. 'Hollis said he has a special night planned! He must have good news for me!'

"She gulped her breakfast and left for school. That was the last time I saw her happy."

Momo looked off into the distance as she continued the story. Nora left that evening to meet Hollis for her birthday dinner. Three hours later, she stomped into the house, muttering under her breath. Momo called her from the living room to join her, but Nora shook her head. She then stormed off to her room and slammed her door.

"I heard her weeping, but Nora wouldn't let me in. She promised she was fine, but she said if Hollis called, she wouldn't talk to him. The phone rang the next morning, but it wasn't Hollis. Lydia called to break the news."

Dorothy found Hollis in the courtyard. It appeared he had been there for hours. Nora told the police she had left a drunk, but conscious, Hollis. She admitted they had argued, but he was alive when she left. Lydia and Dorothy said they heard the courtyard gate open and close around ten and assumed Hollis walked Nora home.

Lydia and Dorothy arranged for Nora to be seated with the family at the funeral. They, along with Momo, assured Nora that she was not to blame for Hollis's death. By the time Nora left New Orleans, she claimed she agreed Hollis had a tragic accident. When Momo took her to the airport, Nora tried to hide her sadness, but her tears flowed as they reached her gate.

"Saying goodbye to Nora broke my heart. I expected to wave her and Hollis off to their future." Momo grabbed a cocktail napkin and dabbed her eyes. "Instead, Nora was leaving on her own. She kept to her plans. As much as she claimed she was all right, I knew she wasn't. Hollis was the love of her life."

I put my hand over Momo's hand. "Did she ever come back to New Orleans before this time?"

"Every few years, she would come to visit. She would stay in a hotel even though I insisted she should stay with me. Dorothy and Lydia offered, too. Nora declared she didn't want to stay in places that had such a mix of bittersweet memories." Momo gave a little laugh. "I told her that was all of New Orleans. We have places with horrible histories and those with happy histories. You can't live one without the other."

I couldn't agree more. Even though I hadn't even been here for a year, I understood firsthand how history, good and bad, was revered here. I still hadn't come to terms with all the bad, but I appreciated all the good that had befallen me in this city.

Momo reached over and put a splash of bourbon in our glasses. She raised the crystal glass to her lips, but put it down. "Sammy, Nora never once lied to me, but she did tonight. Something important is in that card. She didn't just blurt out, 'I knew I shouldn't have killed him' for no reason. I don't want Nora to die with Hollis's death on her conscience."

I joined Momo in taking a sip of our drinks. Momo's concern, perhaps even fear, covered her face. While I had just met Nora, any friend of Momo's was a friend of mine. I would help Momo with this mystery. I just hoped it didn't end with Nora being guilty of murder.

4

"Connor, I don't need two cakes. One is plenty." I wrapped my arms around my boyfriend's waist and looked into his beaming face.

"But we need two of everything if we're going with Aunt Charlene's double theme." Connor pulled me in closer. I snuggled against his black Preservation Hall T-shirt, almost stepping on his vintage tennis shoes. His sandalwood after-shave almost lulled me into relaxing and agreeing with him about the cakes. But I pulled away before I succumbed to his charms.

My morning started with my boyfriend, Connor Tyler, and me discussing my upcoming birthday party. Everyone in Thibodeaux Mansion overruled me when I said a small party would be fine. They insisted we should invite all my friends, but they agreed we would have it here in the court-yard. I've never known a group of people so eager for a birthday party. Then again, people will celebrate for any reason in New Orleans.

"I still don't know why y'all let Aunt Charlene be in

charge. She doesn't understand the concept of a simple party," I said.

My only blood relatives were Charlene St. Martin, who was my father's sister-in-law, and her son, Jasper. While I loved them both, Aunt Charlene had a knack for coming up with wild ideas. So far, I stopped her from hiring a magician, bringing in a mime, and searching for a dance troop to teach us to belly dance. I quashed those ideas, but I let her keep her double theme. I had two birthdays: the date I was born and the one assigned by the Louisiana Department of Children and Family Services when I went into foster care. I only learned of my "real" birthday this year when Aunt Charlene tracked me down. Knowing my actual birthday didn't change anything for me. There was no reason to celebrate both days.

Birthday celebrations were never a big deal to me. They might have been before I turned seven, but I'm not sure. What I remember is the night before my seventh birthday party, my parents broke the news they had adopted me. Apparently, one of my friends overheard our parents talking about my adoption. They decided to tell me before anyone else did.

I appreciated the information, and to me, it didn't make a difference. Ryan and Lorna Richardson were wonderful parents until their deaths two years ago. However, when I went through their things, I found out they had deceived me. All along, they knew I had family left after Hurricane Geoffrey took me away from my parents and brother. My Uncle Preston blackmailed them so he wouldn't tell the authorities I did have family. According to my cousin Jasper and my Aunt Charlene, I had a better life with the Richardsons. I wish I could have known my brother, the only survivor of the hurricane, before we met here in New Orleans.

Connor handed me a cup of coffee, and I inhaled its warm, comforting scent. Chicory coffee with the right amount of creamer was the only way to wake up. "A low-key party with our friends and family is all I want. It's all I need."

"We don't do anything low-key here in New Orleans." Connor laughed. "But I promise we will keep the shenanigans down to a minimum. I nixed your aunt's idea of doing a second line down Royal Street."

"Thank you." I kissed Connor. As a spectator, I enjoyed watching second lines go down Royal Street. Second lines were a parade that included a brass band with participants wearing brightly colored clothes, hats, and waving handkerchiefs. Many danced with parasols as they headed down the street. There didn't need to be a reason for a second line, but many were held after weddings or to celebrate special events or festivals.

While I had joined a few, I didn't want to be the subject of one. That was way too much attention for me. This birthday was already feeling overwhelming, and I still had over a week to go before my party.

"But really, Sammy, what's going on? Your birthday seems to bother you. Or are you thinking about both your families?" Connor put his arm around me, and I leaned my head against him. Connor was a good listener and knew when to give advice and when to listen. But I didn't want to talk about it this morning. I wanted to enjoy my day off with a stop at Cafe Beignet before going to the New Orleans Museum of Art.

Before I brushed off Connor's concerns, I was saved by the bell, or rather, my cell phone. Most of my friends and family texted me, so either it was Andrew or Momo.

"Good morning, Momo." While my tone was cheerful, my body tensed. Had something happened overnight to Nora? "Is everything okay?"

"Oh, yes. I didn't mean to worry you," Momo said. "Nothing is wrong except Paige left her medicine bag here."

"Is that a problem? I recall Paige saying today was her day off." I mouthed goodbye to Connor as he left the apartment. Nubi took his spot by me, but on top of the kitchen counter.

"Well, no. But what if she needs it for another client? I'd hate for her not to have it."

"Momo, you said she was in between jobs." I stifled a laugh. "You want me to drop it off and see if I can convince her to talk about Nora, right?"

"No, no. I thought if you were going out this morning, you could go by. Lady Clementine, stop playing with that cord!" I heard the phone drop onto the floor. Momo was my only friend with a landline. She also had a cell phone, but I imagined she kept the landline just for Lady Clementine to play with. "Sorry, Sammy. That cat can't keep herself away from the phone cord."

"Are you sure she's not calling you out for your true intentions?" I didn't hold back my laughter this time. "I'm happy to take the bag and chat with Paige."

Momo and I ended our call, and I quickly gathered my backpack. Nubi rushed out the front door toward the back courtyard wall. In a flash, my black cat jumped up and over into the neighbor's courtyard. I had no idea what he was investigating. But I did know I was on my way to investigate Nora's past.

5

———

"Sammy, thanks so much for coming over." Momo opened her door before I reached the top step. "I hope Paige will talk to you this morning. Nora is not herself."

"Oh, no. What happened?"

Momo reached for a black medicine bag by her feet and handed it to me. I stepped back as she came outside and closed the door behind it. Momo's gray hair hung loosely over her shoulders, and she wasn't wearing her usual mascara or lipstick. My concern grew as I noticed the dark circles under her eyes and her sallow skin.

"I could hear Nora tossing and turning all night. She called out around two a.m." Momo wrapped her thin arms around her body. "When I reached her room, she was crying and saying, 'I'm sorry, Hollis.' It just broke my heart."

I pulled Momo into a quick embrace. She stepped back and wiped her eyes. "Don't mind this old woman's sentimentality. I was the one who told Nora that Hollis had died. Watching her last night was like we were both reliving that dreadful evening."

"I wish I had never found that card," I said.

'No, I'm glad you found Hollis's card. I believe everything happens for a reason. Yes, I do." Momo smiled through her tears. "Obviously, this has burdened her for all these years. But I don't believe she had anything to do with Hollis's death."

"Has she said anything else to you this morning?"

Momo shook her head. "She claims she doesn't remember what she said last night. That it was the painkillers talking."

"Don't you believe her?"

"I want to, but she seems preoccupied this morning. It's pointless to make her talk. She's as stubborn as a dog with a bone."

"That reminds me of another person I know."

"Whatever do you mean?" Momo laughed and hugged me.

"Did she show you the card yet?" I asked.

"No. Believe me, I tried." Momo sighed. "I considered sneaking the drawer open to get to it, but I didn't. Invading her privacy isn't right no matter how curious I am."

"I'd have a hard time not looking at it either. But I bet she'll show it to you soon," I said.

"You're a sweetheart to do this for this stubborn old dog. Keep an eye on Lydia and especially Dorothy."

"Why?" The ladies seemed mild-mannered to me yesterday. Well, until Nora opened the card.

"Lydia constantly asks for donations for whatever charity-of-the-month she's into. And Dorothy is always looking for a wife for her son, Emerson." Momo's disdain came through loud and clear. "Now, you're probably thinking I'm being snarky, but if you talk to either of them, you'll understand why I warned you."

My curiosity was piqued, and I wanted to run into Lydia and Dorothy. Was that Momo's intention, or was she simply giving me a heads-up about them? Either way, I wouldn't shy away from them if they were there.

I studied the Davenport home from across the street. From my friend Neal Bennett's French Quarter architecture tours, I recognized it as a four-bay redbrick Creole cottage. Gray shingles covered the roof, and white frames surrounded two dormer windows.

Deep-green shutters covered three doorways, except the last on the far left. Brick stairs led to the door, so I assumed this was the entrance. I crossed the street, heading toward the unshuttered doorway. The courtyard entrance caught my eye as I waited for someone to answer the doorbell. Painted the same color as the shutters, it featured a lion door knocker. Curved bars on the top of the doorframe deterred anyone from climbing over the door. The only nod to the modern age was the electric keypad in place of a regular lock.

If no one answered the front door, I would try that one. Sometimes, houses had alley-only entrances. Before I had the chance to ring a second time, Paige's mother opened the door. Her gray hair was pulled into a ponytail and she wore a white tennis dress with a matching sweater tied over her shoulders.

"Hello. Can I help you?" Lydia Townsend studied my face. "You're Momo's friend, aren't you? We met last night."

"Yes. I'm Samantha Richardson. Paige left her bag, and Momo asked me to return it."

"How thoughtful. I can give it to her." A large emerald

ring sparkled in the morning sun as she reached out for the bag.

"Momo wanted me to ask Paige a few questions. May I see her?" I held tight to the bag.

"Questions about what?" Lydia pursed her lips.

"She wondered if there was anything she could do for Nora today. After last night's revelation, Momo is worried about her," I said.

"Finding that card from Hollis was shocking for all of us," Lydia snapped, but quickly changed her tone. "I realize Nora was particularly upset since the card was addressed to her. Has she said anything more about it?"

I shook my head. "I haven't spoken to her, but Momo said she hadn't."

"Perhaps she will later." A look of annoyance flashed across her face, but she smiled. "Let's go find Paige. She lives in the guesthouse in the back."

I entered through the small foyer. To my right was a modern kitchen with maple cabinets and gleaming stainless-steel appliances. We entered the dining room and living room. A floor-to-ceiling brick fireplace, open on both sides, defined the spaces. The living room looked perfect, with traditional furniture, flowers, and lamps.

At first, though, it appeared impersonal, like a photograph from a home magazine, but then a table filled with silver frames drew my attention. I recognized the sisters in their younger days, laughing with a handsome young man. I assumed it was Hollis and understood why Nora fell in love with him. The siblings all shared sparkling eyes and slim noses, but Hollis had an extra spark. I couldn't quite place it. It must be that X factor people talk about.

He towered over his sisters by at least a foot. He had his arms around them and a grin that drew me in. The sisters were also smiling. The photo revealed their obvious close-ness. I couldn't deny a moment of jealousy hit me. Being an only child without cousins, I never experienced that family bond. By the time I discovered I had a sibling, the chance for a happy relationship had already vanished.

We passed the dining room table set for eight with pink and green floral china, sparkling silverware, and crystal glasses.

"You have a lovely home, Mrs. Townsend," I said to the back of Lydia's head.

She didn't turn around, but she acknowledged with a quick, "Thank you."

The wood floor transitioned to tile as we entered the last room, which appeared to be a conservatory with brown wicker chairs and flowerpots of varying sizes. A mix of strong floral scents filled the air. Each side of the room had a steep staircase to the second floor. The back wall featured two sets of French doors, allowing a view of the brick court-yard. Fifty feet away on the other side of the courtyard stood a white stucco two-story house with dark green shutters and a balcony across the top floor.

"Paige lives in Hollis's house. I mean, the guesthouse." Lydia's hand slipped off the door handle. She wiped her hand on her skirt and grasped the handle again. She turned around to face me. "I'm not sure how much you know, but Hollis died in the courtyard."

"Momo told me. It must be difficult to go outside," I said.

"It is, but I also feel closer to him here. We had such good times as children in the courtyard." Lydia's eyes watered. "From the lack of an accent, I assume you haven't grown up in the South. We still talk about those we've lost, like they're still here."

"You're right, I didn't grow up here. But I learned quickly that the past and present are intertwined here," I said.

"That's an excellent way to describe it." Lydia's face softened. "No one ever truly leaves us. We're connected differently, that's all."

I took in a deep breath as Lydia opened the door. Entering a place where a death had occurred didn't scare me. I just couldn't imagine passing the place every day where a loved one had died. Did it become easier as time passed? I'm not sure I would feel that way, especially if it were my home.

I heard the sounds of trickling water as I followed Lydia outside. To my right, ivy covered the brick wall. I turned left and found the source of the sound. Water spouted into a circular basin from a relief of a man's face on the ivy wall. Two square planting beds with lush green bushes and plants flanked each side.

But there was something odd about the water fountain. A young woman lay draped over the edge. For a moment, I considered she was searching for something in the fountain. The awkward position of her legs and the stillness of her body erased that idea.

I rushed over to the fountain where the water sprayed onto the woman's damp hair. The basin emitted a metallic odor as the reddish-brown water swirled around the woman's face. I didn't need to turn her over to recognize her. She wore the same scrubs as last night. The only thing different was the large wound on the back of her head.

Paige Townsend's dead body lay in the courtyard, just like her uncle over forty years ago.

6

———

"Paige! Get up!" Lydia now stood next to me. She grasped her daughter's right shoulder and tried to flip her over. Her hands shook, making it impossible for her to grip her firmly.

"Let me do this." I slid Lydia aside. The large wound on Paige's head made me want to gasp, but I bit my lip to keep quiet. I rolled her onto her back and checked for a pulse. Between the additional wound on her forehead and the stiffness of her body, I didn't expect to find one.

"Is she dead?" Lydia placed her hand on Paige's cheek. She withdrew her hand as if she had received an electric shock. And then she screamed, her voice growing louder with each sob. I put my arm around her shoulders to steady her, but also to keep focused on the situation at hand. I fought back the tears welling up to keep Lydia calm.

"Mrs. Townsend, why don't you sit at the table while I call the police?" I tried to walk her to one of the outdoor chairs on the other side of the courtyard. She wouldn't move. She froze like a statue of a woman caught in the most agonizing moment of her life, which this must have been.

The back door flew open, and Dorothy stomped out of the house. Wearing a white tennis skirt and jacket, she beelined to a sobbing Lydia.

"What in the tarnation is wrong with you? We're going to be late for our match." Dorothy lifted Lydia's chin. "Did something happen to that cat of yours?"

Lydia pointed to Paige's body.

"Oh, no. No, no, no!" Dorothy dashed over to the water fountain in her bare feet. I ran behind her, afraid that she would slip on the wet tiles. There was no need, since her feet stayed firmly on the ground.

"Mrs. Merritt, I'm sorry but there is nothing we can do. We should leave Paige here for the police," I said.

"Who are you? What are you doing here?" Dorothy grabbed my arm, making me flinch from the force she used.

"That's Momo's friend from last night, Samantha Richardson." Lydia stumbled over to us.

Dorothy released her grip and took a step back from me. I rubbed my arm, hoping there wouldn't be a bruise underneath my sweater. Given the circumstances, I didn't have the heart to be angry with Dorothy.

"Yes, of course." Dorothy turned to her sister. "What happened to Paige? Did she fall? Have you called for an ambulance?"

"Mother, what is going on out here?" The booming voice belonged to a tall man wearing a navy-blue suit that hung off his shoulders. Stubble, matching his graying hair, covered his slim face. As he walked around the planters, he stopped dead in his tracks. "Is that Paige? What happened?"

"Emerson, she's dead." Dorothy collapsed against her son's chest.

Lydia wailed again. I considered going over and hugging Lydia as her sobs racked her body. Dorothy had her son, but

Lydia had just lost her daughter. Before I could decide to go over to her, Emerson left his mother and quickly embraced Lydia.

"Mother, take Aunt Lydia inside. Have you called the police?" said Emerson.

"I can do that," I said.

The three looked startled at the sound of my voice. It felt like I was invisible.

"Excuse me, but who are you?" Emerson left his mother and aunt and came over to me. "Did you do this?"

My mouth went dry as he came too close to my personal space. I couldn't quite place his expression. Was he suspicious of me or just confused? I slipped my hand in my pocket, ready to call the police. Hopefully, it would just be to report Paige's death and not a physical altercation with this man.

"I'm Samantha Richardson. Momo McBride asked me to return Paige's medical bag." I pointed to the bag I had dropped ten feet away from the fountain. "Your aunt was taking me to see Paige when we found her here."

"Is this true, Aunt Lydia?" Emerson looked at me instead of his aunt. I wanted to tell him I wasn't a liar, but I refrained. The situation he walked into that included a complete stranger called for a bit of suspicion, to say the least.

"Yes, it is." Lydia clutched her stomach. "Can someone please call the authorities? I think I'm going to be sick."

Dorothy rushed to her sister and escorted her inside the house. "Emerson, call the police."

"Don't go anywhere." Emerson pointed his cell phone at me. He turned his back to me before I could say I had no plans to leave.

While he was on his cell phone, I looked around the

water fountain. "I'm so sorry, Paige," I whispered to her lifeless body. Although she wasn't the first dead body I had seen, it was still difficult. She wore the same clothes she did at Momo's house yesterday. Besides the wound on the back of her head and her forehead, she didn't have any other visible marks. When I flipped her over, one left arm had been in the water and the other tucked under her body. Her right hand was clenched, and something stuck out from her grip. I knew better than to pull it out. Considering how stiff her body felt, I doubted I could get it out even if I tried.

The consequences of doing it wouldn't be worth the wrath of the police. Especially if Christine Gammon and Rob Armstrong were assigned to this case. I expected they would be. They were the best detectives in the NOPD and known for handling difficult as well as high-profile cases. By the way Emerson was throwing his name around on the phone, he definitely acted as if he were an important person in the city.

I moved back to stand by Paige's medical bag as Emerson finished his phone call. He came over to me with his hand outstretched.

"Please accept my apologies for my behavior. The scene was confusing." He shook my hand with little effort. "I'm Emerson Merritt. So you are a friend of Paige's?"

Emerson's businesslike demeanor surprised me. Wasn't he upset that his cousin was dead? Then again, he might be keeping his emotions in check for the sake of the family.

Once again, I explained why I was here and who I was. He listened to me, but his eyes remained glued to the water fountain. "I'm sorry you have to see your cousin this way."

Emerson pulled at the collar of his shirt as if it was choking him. He then turned his attention back to me. "Thank you. Paige was a lovely young woman with a bright future ahead of her. She'll leave a hole in our family. Just like Uncle Hollis."

Was Paige's death just like her uncle's death forty-three years ago? As the sound of sirens grew closer, I couldn't help but wonder if Nora's declaration about the past was intertwined with the future.

7

———

"It's not a crime scene if you aren't here, is it, Sammy?" Christine Gammon gave me her usual exasperated look as she joined me in the courtyard. She pulled out a notebook and pen from the pocket of her beige trench coat. Her jacket covered a black blouse and pants with a matching pair of boots.

"Christine, I have a good excuse to be here."

"Oh, I'm sure you do. You always do," she said. "But really, what's going on? Someone reported a woman found dead at the Davenport House. The police officer called it in as a possible homicide."

I explained I came here at Momo's request to return Paige's medical bag. I didn't tell her that Momo wanted me to speak with Paige about Nora and Hollis. If someone murdered Paige, her involvement in last night's conversation would become important. But I didn't want to muddy the waters, especially since Paige's death might be an accident. My gut told me it was murder. The multiple wounds and the piece of paper in her clenched fist gave me pause.

"Lydia's hands were shaking, so I turned Paige over.

Besides the wound on the back of her head, there was a deep gash on her forehead. She appeared to be in rigor, but I checked for a pulse to make sure." My morning coffee churned in my stomach. No matter how many dead bodies I had found, it still shook me to my core.

"Sammy, how are you?" Detective Rob Armstrong strode toward us and put his arm around me. I rested against him and my nerves settled. While his muscular frame and tall height may seem imposing to some, especially criminals, to me, it was a comfort. Not only were his hugs soothing, his ability to listen and offer sage advice reassured me in good times and bad times.

"Fine, I guess," I said. "I'm better than Paige's family. They moved inside after Emerson called the police."

"Yes, we all are better off." Rob looked at Paige's body. "Let's go check out the scene, Christine. Sammy, please wait here."

I stood alone like a wallflower at a school dance. Having been at a few crime scenes, I knew to stay put until Rob or Christine came back. But it didn't keep me from studying the courtyard. The brick wall on the right side was at least twenty feet high, making it difficult for anyone to climb over them. If the killer had a ladder, it would be possible, but it was a long jump down. The wall on the left, behind the fountain, matched in height, but the next town house's wall was directly beside it. If a ladder wasn't dropped from the third-floor window, then no one from that town house could have entered the courtyard.

The guesthouse took up the entire back wall of the courtyard, so no one came in that way. Common sense would say her killer either came in by invitation through the courtyard gate or through the house. Perhaps the murderer forced their way inside, but I didn't notice any defensive wounds on Paige's hands. I might be mistaken, but Paige seemed like the type to fight back. Perhaps it was someone she let into the courtyard. Paige wasn't wearing her coat from last night, so I wondered if she had been inside her home and then came out. But where was she going?

My mind buzzed with questions, but no answers...yet. I already knew Momo would ask me to find answers for her and Nora. But in the meantime, I just had to stay in my spot until Rob and Christine came back. They left the water fountain, so I hoped they were coming my way. If they had been, the opening of the back door distracted them.

Emerson came out first, with a scowl on his face. "Who's in charge here?"

"Don't use that tone, Emerson." Dorothy came out from behind him now wearing socks and tennis shoes. "We're not at a restaurant complaining about cold food. The police are doing their job."

Emerson turned red. "Yes, Mother, I realize that. But the detectives should have come to us first. Aunt Lydia doesn't need to be back here."

Wrapped in a gray shawl, Lydia stepped out of the door. With her face toward the fountain, she rubbed her red eyes. "Is my baby still here?"

Crossing the courtyard in large strides, Rob approached Lydia first. "Mrs. Townsend, I am sorry for your loss. Let's sit down at the table before we speak."

Rob led Lydia over to the table and pulled out a chair for her. Robotically, she sat down and stared at the table. Emerson escorted his mother and sat her next to her sister. He hovered over both of them.

"I apologize for not coming to see you sooner. My name is Detective Rob Armstrong, and this is my partner, Detective Christine Gammon."

"We are sorry for your loss." Christine joined Rob. "Ms. Richardson has told us what happened, but we need to ask you a few questions when you are ready."

I hurried to the group before Christine could stop me. Once again, the family stared at me as if I had just appeared from thin air.

"Are you all right, Samantha? I'm sorry we haven't even offered you coffee," Lydia said.

"Th-there is no need, but thank you," I stammered. The last thing Lydia needed to do was offer me coffee. Perhaps she was just on autopilot, but I doubt I'd be that hospitable in her condition.

"Speaking of coffee, Mrs. Townsend, why don't you go inside with Mrs. Merritt and Mr. Merritt? Officer Banks will be happy to make tea or coffee for you. Detective Gammon and I will be in as soon as possible."

Officer Banks, who was within earshot, stepped toward the back door. "Let me help you get settled inside while you wait for the detectives."

"Yes, that would be helpful. Thank you." Dorothy stood up first and offered her hand to her sister. Hand in hand, the sisters followed Officer Banks inside the house.

"Detectives, I believe I should stay out here as a representative of the family." Emerson hadn't moved, even when his mother waved him to the door.

"That's very thoughtful of you, but your family needs you right now." Rob's voice was kind, but firm. "We'll continue gathering evidence, and we'll remove your cousin's body. You don't want to be here for that. Detective Gammon and I will join you shortly."

Emerson rubbed his chin with his hand. "I need to tell you about Paige's ex-boyfriend, Tate King. Aunt Lydia will say he would never hurt Paige, but I have my doubts."

"Why is that?" Rob took out his notebook and pen.

"They argued all the time. I could hear them in the main house even when they were inside Paige's house." Emerson pointed toward the guesthouse in the back.

"That must have been quite loud," Rob said. "So you live in the main house, along with your mother and aunt?"

Emerson turned pink. "Just temporarily. I'm looking for a new place."

If what Momo said was true about Dorothy always looking for a wife for Emerson, living with his mother couldn't help the situation.

"Did you hear anything last night?" Christine asked.

"No, but I wasn't home until midnight. I had a business meeting that ran late, so I went straight to bed when I came home," Emerson said. "My bedroom is on the second floor, looking over the street."

"Have your mother and your Aunt Lydia lived here long?" Rob said.

"Yes. It has been our family home for decades." Emerson bristled with indignation. "My mother and aunt grew up in the house. My mother and father moved in with my grand-parents when I was a baby. Lydia moved in when her husband died four years ago. Paige has lived in the guest-house for just a year."

"Mr. Merritt, who has access to the courtyard?" Christine pointed to the garden door. "I noticed it has a keypad. I own the same brand, and I'm aware that it records who enters. Would you mind showing it to me?"

Emerson stared vacantly for a moment, but then pulled out his cell phone. He opened an app and showed it to Christine. "Here you go. That last number is Paige's. The other number is for the gardener at two in the afternoon yesterday."

I tried to lean discreetly toward Emerson's phone, but Rob cleared his throat. I took the hint and stepped back, but I noted the time for Paige's last entry, 10:30 p.m. Paige's killer either entered with her or was already there. Or it could have been someone who came through the house. Could Lydia or Dorothy be the killer? Imagining Lydia, in particular, was difficult. Emerson seemed more likely than his mother and aunt, but he was cooperating. Then again, many murderers do.

"Thank you, Mr. Merritt." Christine closed her notebook and crossed her arms. "We appreciate your help, and we'll join your family shortly."

Emerson nodded and strode toward the back door. Before he opened the door, he turned his head toward the fountain. He stopped as they zipped Paige into a body bag. The bustling atmosphere of crime scene workers, police officers, and the detectives changed to one of silence. The only sounds were the lifting of Paige's body onto the gurney and the water trickling into the fountain. Emerson wiped his eyes and dashed inside as the investigators rolled Paige out of the courtyard.

As soon as Emerson closed the door, Rob focused on me. "Okay. What did you see when you came outside with Mrs. Townsend? I understand someone moved Paige's body to check if she was alive."

"Yes, I turned her over. Paige was lying over the fountain when we came into the courtyard. I noticed the wound on the back of her head and found the second one when I turned her face up." I shivered at the image in my head. "In her clenched right hand, there appeared to be a piece of paper. Before you ask, I didn't touch it or try to open her hand."

"Yes, you know better than to disturb a crime scene,"

Rob said. "How did Mrs. Townsend react when she saw her daughter?"

"She let out the most gut-wrenching scream. I don't believe she had anything to do with Paige's death. She genuinely seemed shocked at the sight of her daughter," I said.

Rob nodded. "Tell me how you're connected to the family. Christine said Momo sent you here with Paige's medical bag."

"Yes. Paige is, was, Momo's friend's hospice nurse. They'll be devastated by the news. Momo and her friend Nora are friends of the sisters, too."

"Okay, we'll need to talk to them." Rob waved Christine over. "I assume you want to tell Momo and Nora the news, so I'll go with you."

"I can do it myself," I protested. "Naturally, you'll want information from them, but they had nothing to do with Paige's death."

"I just need to speak to them, Sammy. I won't accuse them of murder." Rob put his hand on my shoulder. "Remember, we need to follow the rules, even if we all know each other here."

I sighed. Rob was right, but I dreaded Momo opening the door. While Rob and Christine helped to solve Momo's niece's death, the sight of a detective at your door never meant good news. I experienced that firsthand when my brother was murdered. Nothing makes that heartbreak fully disappear.

"Let's go give her the news." I braced myself to go to tell Nora and Momo about what happened.

8

———————

Although Momo's house was only a few minutes' walk, it felt like hours and miles to get there. Rob and I knew each other well enough that we didn't have to fake small talk. Walking in silence wasn't awkward for us. I appreciated the time I had to gather myself before sharing the horrible news with Momo and Nora.

Rob knocked on the door, which Momo answered within seconds. "Sammy, I've been calling you. Rob, what are you doing here?"

"I'm sorry, Miss Momo, but we have bad news for you and your friend, Nora Winslow. May we come in?" Rob said.

"Yes, but tell me what happened, now." Momo used her arms to block the doorway.

Rob's face fell, but he did as Momo asked. "Paige Townsend was found dead this morning in the Davenport House courtyard."

Momo's arms dropped to her sides, but otherwise, she didn't react. The sounds of pedestrians and cars seemed to grow louder as the three of us stood there.

"Why don't we go inside now?" I grasped Momo's hands.

Momo gestured for us to enter and led us to the kitchen. "I have a feeling we're all going to need coffee."

"Sit down, Momo. I can do this for you." Having made coffee for us before, I opened the cabinet where Momo kept her coffee and mugs. I grabbed the can of Community Coffee, only to find it empty. Behind it, a full carton of half-and-half remained. I threw it away.

"So that's where I put the cream. I blamed Lady Clementine for taking it." Momo's face turned red.

"Meow," Lady Clementine retorted, before settling on the chair next to Rob.

"We've all done that, except perhaps Lady C." Rob scratched her behind the ears. "I don't need coffee, but I appreciate the offer."

"Sammy, will you make tea? Nora will want a cup when she wakes up," Momo said.

Fortunately, the tea supply was in order, and I went about making a pot. As I did, the condition of the kitchen worried me. Momo was always so methodical. Was the stress of taking care of Nora too much for her? Now wasn't the time to ask her. But I made a note to call in a grocery order for her with Frankie. Not only did Frankie Fortuna own the store, she was a good friend of Momo's. If anyone could get Momo to speak, it was her.

As the tea brewed, Rob explained what had happened to Paige. Momo clenched her fist and pressed it against her mouth. While she might have stopped herself from crying out, tears still spilled over her face. I grabbed a box of tissues and placed it in front of Momo.

After wiping her tears, she said, "What happened? Sammy, did you find her?"

"Yes, along with Lydia. I'm so sorry, Momo."

"I'm the one who is sorry. I should have taken the bag to her myself," Momo said.

"Miss Momo, you had Sammy deliver the bag to Paige on her day off. Why?" Rob took out his notebook and pen. "From what I understand, Paige wouldn't have needed her bag today. When was she scheduled to work here next?"

"Tomorrow." Momo pursed her lips together.

"Now, I'm not trying to insult you, Miss Momo, but was there another reason you sent Sammy with a bag Paige didn't need?" Rob's tone was kind but firm.

Momo looked at me as if she wanted me to answer. Lying to Rob felt wrong, but I couldn't share Nora's outburst. Not that I believed Nora had anything to do with Paige's death. Well, except for hiding the card away from everyone. I prayed Paige's death wasn't related to the card, but it couldn't just be ignored.

"Last night I found a card in a book that had been Nora's decades ago."

Momo interrupted me. "It was a card from Nora's boyfriend who died forty-three years ago. He was Paige's uncle. We were surprised, to say the least. Nora didn't want to talk about it to all of us."

"Who was all of us?" Rob asked.

"Me, Sammy, Paige, her mother Lydia, and her aunt Dorothy. Before you ask, only Nora read the card. But it definitely upset her, and I'd hoped Paige could shed light on Nora's true emotional state." Momo kept her eyes fixed on me as she spoke. I interpreted it as her way of saying, *Please don't say anything about Nora's outburst.* I didn't.

"All right." Rob tapped his pen on his notebook. "How was Paige when she left here? Did she seem upset?"

"No. She was like she always was. Paige left at her normal time and met her friend Tate King, down the street."

"Tell me about their relationship. Was it tumultuous?" Rob said.

"Paige and Tate were rekindling their romance, so I doubt he killed her." Nora stood in the kitchen doorway, her hands gripping the sides of her walker. She wore loose black pants and a purple sweater that hung off her shoulders. Her tearstained face appeared paler today than yesterday.

"Nora, I didn't realize you were awake." Momo pushed her chair back and stumbled as she rushed toward her friend. "I'm sorry you had to hear about Paige this way."

"Even with this contraption, I can still sneak around." Nora pulled away from Momo's embrace. "Tell me what happened."

"Miss Nora, why don't you take a seat first?" Rob offered his chair, but Nora waved him away.

"I sit most of the day, so I'll just stand." Nora pulled her shoulders back. "Please tell me how Paige died."

Momo stayed next to Nora as Rob explained what had happened. She tightened her grip on her walker, but she didn't move. Only her chin quivered when Rob finished. "I'm sorry for your loss, Miss Nora. Are you up for answering a few questions?"

Nora nodded. "I don't think I can add anything more to what Momo told you. Paige was perfectly fine when she left me in my room."

"Had the card from her uncle bothered her?" Rob said.

"Not at all. Just surprised, like all of us. Right, Momo? Right, Sammy?"

"As far as I can tell, yes," I said. Momo just nodded.

"So I can't imagine how any of this is related to her death. Do you really believe she was murdered?" Nora bit her lip.

"It could have been an accident, but we need to gather as

much information as we can." Rob stood up and placed his hand on Nora's. "Anything you can share about Paige is helpful."

"If I think of anything else, I'll call," Nora murmured.

"I'd appreciate that. Again, I'm sorry for your loss, Miss Nora." Rob put his business card on the kitchen table. "I can see myself out. Call me if you need anything at all, Miss Momo. I'll see you later, Sammy." Rob gave one of my shoulders a quick squeeze and left the kitchen.

After the front door closed, Nora turned around and headed out of the kitchen. "Momo, I need to go to Lydia right now."

"Nora, I don't think that's such a good idea. There must be so much going on at the house," Momo said. "Let's wait until the evening, at least to call them."

"No, we should go to Lydia. She's just lost her daughter and will need support." Nora didn't turn to face us, but said, "When Hollis died, Lydia and Dorothy supported me. I should do the same for them."

"Nora will crawl to their house if I don't take her." Momo sighed.

"I heard that!" Nora called out from the hallway. "And you're right, Momo. I'm getting my purse from my bedroom, then I'll meet you at the front door."

Nora continued down the hall, her walker echoing off the hardwood floor. Momo flopped into a kitchen chair, resting her head in her hands. "There's no way Nora can walk to the Davenport House. I'm not certain I can push Nora in her wheelchair. With the bumpy sidewalks and streets, I doubt I can do it."

"I'll help you. If I can't push her, I'll call Connor to help." I put my arms around Momo's shoulders. "Where is her wheelchair?"

"It's in the hall closet. Let me go get it and I'll meet you out front." Momo stood up and placed a hand on my cheek. "You're a wonderful friend, Sammy Richardson. I am so thankful God brought you into my life."

"Likewise, Momo McBride." I smiled, hoping it would stop me from crying. Now wasn't the time, but being reminded of how many loving friends I had in my life almost brought me to tears. Now wasn't the time for self-reflection. Momo and Nora needed help.

Momo and I went our separate ways. I knocked on Nora's bedroom door. "Nora, Momo is getting your wheelchair. Can I help you to the front door?"

"Come in, Sammy."

I entered her bedroom. Lady Clementine lay in Nora's lap as she scratched behind the cat's ears. Nora wasn't crying, but her nose remained red.

"I'm so sorry, Nora. Paige meant a lot to you, I imagine," I said.

"She did. Paige had only been a baby when Hollis died, but as an adult, she reminded me so much of him." Nora smiled slightly. "They had the same sense of humor and a powerful love for their family and friends."

Nora patted the space on the bed next to Lady Clementine. I sat down. "It's amazing how some family members are like each other, even if they didn't really know each other."

Aunt Charlene said I had the same smile and nose as my mom and had my dad's red hair. But I wasn't certain if my personality resembled theirs. I wish I remembered anything about them, but I didn't.

"Yes, it is. Our last conversation with Paige was about Hollis. She was such a good listener. Hollis loved her so much." Nora wiped a stray tear off her face. "I'm sorry I didn't get the chance to tell her I loved her, too."

"I'm sure Paige already knew you loved her. You don't always have to speak for people to know your feelings."

Lady Clementine meowed in apparent agreement. "Lady C is quite the furry therapist."

"I agree," I said.

"From what Momo tells me, you're a good listener. And a good problem solver."

"That was kind of Momo."

"Oh, it's the truth if Momo said it. She doesn't compliment anyone out of the goodness of her heart." Nora smiled slightly as she scratched the cat on her head. "She suggested I speak with you about Hollis's card. Honestly, I don't think there's much to say about it."

"If you don't mind me saying, you seemed quite upset when you read the card." I held my breath, hoping I wouldn't offend or anger Nora with the question.

I had not.

"Oh, you're trying to be nice, aren't you?" Nora gave a quick giggle. "I'm a tough old bird, so I can handle your questions. Doesn't mean I'm going to answer them all."

"You and Momo are alike in that way." I smiled. "I just can't help but wonder what Hollis said on that card to upset you. You put it away pretty quickly."

"Seeing a card from your dead boyfriend is shocking. But really, I put it away because I didn't want Lydia or Dorothy to see it," Nora interrupted.

"Why didn't you want Hollis's sisters to see the card?"

"I didn't want them to know Hollis was leaving New Orleans after all. They've always believed he was going to stay. Momo told you my story, didn't she?"

I nodded. "She did. I'm so sorry you endured that."

Nora pushed herself up off the bed despite Lady Clementine's plaintive meow. "That happened ages ago.

Now, if you'll excuse me, I need to put my face on. I'll meet you outside."

She moved toward her dresser and took out her makeup bag. Our conversation had ended, according to Nora. I wanted to ask her why she said she shouldn't have killed him, but I left. The front door stood open. At first, I was worried Momo forgot to shut it, but she was outside unfolding the wheelchair.

"Momo, let me get that for you," I said.

"I can do this much. I just don't know if I can get her there in this thing." Beads of sweat formed on Momo's forehead.

"Let me do it." I discreetly tried to look at my watch to see how late I would be to work. But I wouldn't leave Momo alone to take Nora there.

"Sammy, I know you need to get to the shop. I'll figure something out." Momo put on a brave face, but I could see the anxiety in her eyes.

"Let me call Connor. If he can't do it, I'm sure Jasper or Neal could help." Before I could get my cell phone out, a woman with the most Southern drawl I'd ever heard called out.

"Sammy, darling! Your Aunt Charlene is here!"

9

"Aunt Charlene, I didn't realize you were in town already."

When I first met my aunt, my birth father's sister-in-law, she overwhelmed me. Not just with her penchant for brightly colored floral dresses and strongly scented citrus perfume, but with her constant chatter. Much of her talk was about my birth family and calling me by birth name, Sarah Jane.

But over the months, she had a lighter touch with her perfume. She learned to call me Sammy, but she still talked about my birth family. Yes, I appreciated learning my history, but at times it overwhelmed me. Hearing about the people and life I lost after Hurricane Geoffrey also gave me a deep sense of loss. The chain reactions from that event had ended with the death of my brother. But I was fortunate to have my aunt and my cousin Jasper in my life. But the melancholy still comes and goes.

"I was coming to find you!" Charlene hugged me as her citrus perfume wafted from her.

"I was..."

"Now, look at you! Pretty as a picture as always. Glad you're not letting your upcoming birthday keep you down." She sighed deeply as she shook her head. "You're still young enough to have a baby. But not for too long."

I bit my tongue instead of snapping back that turning thirty-one was not grounds for being depressed. My aunt often brought up my "advancing" age and her concern that soon I would be too old to have children. I learned not to argue with her. Between the era and the community she grew up in, getting married and having babies was the norm for women in their early twenties, not my upcoming age of thirty-one.

"Jasper and I thought you were coming to town on Wednesday," I said. "Does he know you're here already?"

"I couldn't wait any longer to be with my family!" Charlene had a smile plastered on her face, but there was a sadness in her eyes. This was the first Thanksgiving without her daughter, Scarlett.

"We're happy to you're here. Everyone will be thrilled to see you early." I hugged her. "Let me introduce you to Myrtle McBride."

"Oh, I know who you are!" Aunt Charlene exclaimed. "Sammy has told me all about you. My son has, too. I'm so glad we're finally meeting!"

"It's wonderful to meet you in person, Mrs. St. Martin. Sammy is a wonderful friend to me as well as your son, Jasper," Momo smiled.

"Oh, now, call me Charlene, please. I'm so glad my babies have a good friend in you." Aunt Charlene looked like a proud parent at a teacher conference.

"I feel the same way about them. Now you must call me Momo. I'd invite you in for coffee, but we're unfortunately off to see our friends. There's been a death in the family."

Aunt Charlene grabbed both of Momo's hands. "Oh, my, I'm sorry. Sammy and I have dealt with our fair share of loss. Your friends will appreciate your support, I'm sure."

Momo stared down at their clasped hands, but didn't let go. "Thank you, Charlene. Now we need to get Nora to our friends' house."

"Is it far away?" Charlene took her hands back and opened her huge purse and pulled out her pink rhinestone encrusted cell phone. "I can call a cab for y'all."

"No, we can walk there, but Nora is in a wheelchair."

"Those bumpy sidewalks and streets are a pain, but I can help you. And Sammy, too, I'm sure." Charlene said.

"Are you sure? Nora isn't heavy, but it's still difficult to maneuver the wheelchair. And Sammy really should get to work." Momo asked what I was about to say. Aunt Charlene didn't strike me as the pushing-a-wheelchair type. She always complained if she had to walk over two blocks in the Quarter.

"Don't you worry, I have experience. After pushing my memaw all around the farm, this will be a piece of cake. I trained in cotton fields. Trust me, it was easier than taking her around the casinos in Arkansas." Charlene laughed.

"Well, I won't say no to an experienced wheelchair driver." Momo's whole body relaxed. "Here's Nora now. Charlene St. Martin, meet my friend, Nora Winslow."

Nora had used her walker to reach the door, but she left it inside the hallway as she walked out onto the steps. Charlene rushed up the stairs and offered her arm to Nora.

"Hello, Nora! I'm Sammy's aunt. Let me say how sorry you've lost someone. But I'm here to help."

"Oh, why, thank you." Nora accepted her arm as she looked quizzically at me and Momo.

"Let's get you settled. Momo, make sure the brake is on

before Nora sits down." Aunt Charlene walked down the steps with Nora.

"Charlene has offered to help us go to the Davenport House," Momo said. "Sammy needs to open up her shop, but Charlene showed up just in time."

"God always knows where you're needed," Charlene said. "Now, Nora, if you need my help to sit down, just say so. My memaw's nurse told me to let her do what she could instead of assuming."

"Your memaw's nurse sounds like Paige. She always says, I mean, said, to tell her to stop when I could do something." Nora dropped into the wheelchair, but the brake held firm.

"So, that's who passed away? I'm so sorry. Let's get you to the house lickety-split." Aunt Charlene adjusted Nora's feet into the holders. "Are you warm enough?"

"I'm ready. Thank you." Nora folded her hands in her lap. "Momo, thanks for finding the wheelchair. And Sammy, thank you for having a kind aunt. We need to go that way."

Charlene pushed Nora past me but stopped to say, "I'll see you later, Sammy. We can catch up then." She kissed me on the cheek and continued on down the street.

"Well, isn't your Aunt Charlene a delightful surprise?" Momo said. "From the look on your face, I'd say you didn't know all that about her."

I nodded. She was right. I had no idea Aunt Charlene took care of her grandmother. She also seemed to have medical skills that she had never mentioned. Apparently, my aunt still had a few stories still to tell me about her. Hopefully, Nora would want to share her past with me, too.

10

———

"Can we sit in the courtyard?" I asked the host as we entered the Grapevine restaurant.

"Really? You're not wearing a parka, so you might freeze." Andrew's light-blue eyes stared at me with concern, but there was a smile on his face. As a former New Yorker, Andrew Ballard enjoyed teasing me about my cold-weather issues. Even though he had lived in the French Quarter for close to fifteen years, he still could withstand the fifty degree weather, like it was a warm spring day. His lightweight gray cashmere sweater was a testament to his ability to handle the cooler temperatures. Unlike me wearing my wool black cardigan over a long-sleeve shirt.

"I'll survive if we sit by a patio heater." I laughed.

No matter the weather, I loved sitting in the restaurant's courtyard. Large slate tiles covered the patio dotted with black metal tables and chairs. Small white lights covered the green umbrellas positioned around the area. A large, round two-tier water fountain splashed water when the wind blew just right.

"Perfect. Thanks so much," I said. The host seated us at a table in the rear of the courtyard.

The warmth of the heater was just what I needed as the chat we were going to have chilled me to the bone. At first, the sound of the cascading water invoked memories of Paige this morning, but I was glad for the privacy. The restaurant catered to locals and tourists, and I didn't want either group overhearing our conversation.

"First, let me say, you did an amazing job curating the books from the estate sale. Considering the morning you had, you didn't need to complete the task today," Andrew said.

After leaving Aunt Charlene in charge of taking Nora and Momo to the Davenport House, I went straight to Lagniappe Books. As curious as I was, I needed to work instead of hearing more details about Paige's death. With Thanksgiving approaching, the bookshop was heading into its biggest season.

"We're partners, so I can't leave you to do all this on your own. Although, I know you did before," I said.

"I did, but I never had the sales we've had, the last months. The addition of new authors, the newsletter, and your excellent salesmanship has revived the shop." Andrew smiled at me like a proud father.

"Thanks for believing in me." I could feel my face turn red. When I moved to New Orleans I never imagined I would be the co-owner of a bookshop. My inheritance from my adopted parents made it possible.

"I always will. Now, are you ready to talk about this morning, or would you rather talk business first?"

"Business, but first a cocktail," I said.

Our server came over and took our drink orders, a Pimm's Cup for me and a Sazerac for Andrew. My favorite cocktail was soothing with lemonade mixed in with the Pimm's syrup. I liked the slight herbal flavor that didn't have a strong alcohol taste like the whiskey in a Sazerac. Although after the morning I had at the Davenport House, a stronger drink might have been in order.

By the time our entrées arrived, we had finished our business chat about the shop. Instead of jumping into talking about my morning at the Davenport House, we decided to enjoy our meal first. I appreciated eating without talking about Paige's death. The vision of Paige lying over the edge of the fountain rarely left my mind. There was never a good time for anyone to die, but around the holidays just seemed to make it worse.

"Are you saving room for dessert?" Andrew asked as I placed my knife and fork onto my plate.

The rich flavor of the duck breast with a blackberry reduction satisfied my stomach that I didn't even need the broccoli and potatoes served with it. But since they were perfectly roasted with just the right amount of heat, I ate some of them, too. I would have my leftovers for breakfast or lunch tomorrow—assuming Connor didn't come by and snag them. He was the one who introduced me to this restaurant, so I wouldn't fault him for wanting my leftovers.

"Yes, I want dessert. Sissy will be joining us in a little bit. Sounds like she needs a crème brûlée after her shift at the hospital." I put my cell phone back down. Normally I wouldn't have kept my phone out during a meal, but I wanted to be available if Momo called.

Momo had phoned in the afternoon to let me know they hadn't gone to the Davenport House after all. "We made it two blocks, and then Nora asked to go home. She didn't come right out and say it, but I believe the thought of going back to Hollis's home was too much," she had said. Momo raved about how helpful Aunt Charlene had been and that they were going to have a drink tonight. At least a friendship came out of today.

"Have you heard anything else from Momo?" Andrew asked.

"No. I imagine she's been comforting Nora this evening. From what she said this afternoon, Nora vacillates between grief and anger." I smoothed the linen napkin in my lap. "If it turns out to be murder, and it's related to Hollis's card, I don't how Nora will handle that."

"If?" Andrew tilted his head. "From what you said this morning, I thought you were positive it was murder."

The server interrupted us to take our dessert order. After he left, I said, "Yes, I do think her death is suspicious. But if it is murder, it had to be someone Paige let into the courtyard or someone who lives in the house. But no one seems to have a motive."

"Maybe Sissy will have some insight from Rob." Andrew pointed over my shoulder. Sissy Covington strolled into the courtyard catching the attention of the other diners. It wasn't just her long blonde hair framing her beautiful face that made her a standout, but the positive energy she exuded. She smiled and said hello to those she knew. I rarely went anywhere with Sissy that she didn't know at least five people.

"Sammy, honey, let me give you a hug." Sissy pulled me out of my chair and into a tight embrace. "I know this wasn't your first time finding someone, but it never gets easier, does it?"

As a nurse, Sissy was no stranger to death. Not only was she good at comforting patients and their families, she did the same for her friends.

"No, it doesn't," I said.

"Thanks, Andrew." Sissy kissed him on the cheek and then sat down in the chair he pulled out for her. "Did I miss dessert already?"

"We just ordered. What would you like? I'll tell our server on my way to the restroom," Andrew said,

"Crème brûlée, of course. I'm sure Sammy ordered one, but I'm not sharing." Sissy grinned. "Oh, and a glass of wine. Whatever they think goes with the dessert. I'm not picky tonight."

Andrew left us to catch up on our day. I insisted Sissy go first. Even with her cheerful demeanor, I could see exhaustion in her eyes.

"Oh, it was a normal day. Well, as normal as it can be at the hospital." Sissy took my glass of water and took a sip. "I hate, just hate, when we have kids as patients. It's the parents that make it harder. They hate feeling useless."

"I can only imagine. I'm sorry it was a tough day." I squeezed Sissy's hand. "Are you off tomorrow?"

"Yes, thank goodness. I plan to stay home all day and start to read one of those books you gave me."

"I'm glad you like mysteries as much as I do. Fictional ones, that is." I grinned.

"Oh, please, you're good at solving the real ones, too. But don't you let Rob know I said that."

"Speaking of Rob, have you heard anything else about Paige's death?" I asked.

"Not really. He called me to say you had found a body, but you were okay." Sissy drummed her fingers on the table. "You should have texted me first. I prefer to hear from you that you're all right. But I understand you were busy."

"I'm sorry." Andrew had given me the same speech when I arrived at the shop this morning. Momo had called him while she was getting Nora's wheelchair. "Let me tell you what happened."

Andrew returned to the table as I wrapped up my story with Momo calling to say they hadn't gone to the Davenport House after all. "And that's all I know."

"Get ready to learn more. I have some information about Paige." Sissy accepted her wine from the server and drank a little bit. "Paige wasn't a nurse at the rehab. She was a patient."

"How did you find out?" Andrew gave Sissy his best concerned-father look.

"I didn't go snooping in HR files, if that's what you're thinking." Sissy frowned at him. "Paige didn't hide it. Her friends told me she was proud that she took control of her issues. But her mother wanted her to keep quiet about it," Sissy said. "Heaven forbid she sully the family name. That's what she told one of her friends."

"Poor Paige. I wonder if that's where she met her boyfriend, Tate King?" I said.

"They were exes, from what I heard," Sissy said.

"Nora said they were talking about getting back together. Could he have killed Paige because she didn't want to get back together?" I said.

"From what I overheard on the phone, Rob and Christine were going to find him tonight. It sounds like he wasn't answering his cell phone, and it was his day off from his job."

"So there's no point of me going there tonight to talk to him. Did they say were else he might go?"

"Samantha, you are not going to track down a murder suspect tonight." Andrew's voice was stern. "And neither are you going to take Sissy with you. The man might not be a suspect, and you would intrude on his grief. And if he is a suspect, you two don't need to go after him like two hunting dogs."

"Yes, Dad," Sissy and I said in unison. We weren't being snarky. Andrew's concern for us meant the world to me.

"Good. Here is our dessert, and afterward I'm walking you both to your apartment doors." Andrew poised his fork over his bread pudding. "Don't make me call Rob, or worse, Christine."

The tension broke with our laughter and we devoured our desserts in silence. Andrew was right. I couldn't go off asking this man questions. Well, at least not tonight. But I could try tomorrow.

11

"Nubi, as soon as I finish this article, I'll feed you. I promise."

My black cat meowed at me, possibly calling me a liar, since I had already said that to him ten minutes ago. My alarm clock buzzed at six thirty instead of its usual time of seven. I wanted extra time to read the online news about Paige's death.

Fortunately, none of the articles included my name. I learned nothing new except Paige's death was considered suspicious. I wondered what information Rob and Christine needed to call it a homicide. The last article I read was from the website Winston's Whispers. While Winston Briggs was more of a sensationalist than a journalist, he occasionally had good information. As I expected, he called it a homicide and called for more police presence in the French Quarter. If a loved one had killed Paige, more police in the neighborhood wouldn't have helped her.

I finally dragged myself out of bed to get ready for the day. Feeding Nubi was my first priority, though.

"See, I'm feeding you before I make my coffee." I

66

scratched Nubi on the little white spot of fur on his head. "And you know I desperately need caffeine in the morning."

Nubi swished his tail until I placed his dish before him. Owning a cat for the first time, everything he did made me smile. Actually, he owned me. I wouldn't even make Connor coffee before my own, as he pointed out on the days he joined me for breakfast. "He's your number one man." Connor would pick Nubi up and hold him like a baby. "I just can't compete with your adorableness."

I made another cup of coffee to take with to work this morning. Going to get coffee and beignets was not an option. We had so much to do to get ready for Black Friday. Although we didn't run big sales like the chain stores, we offered a few specials. But Saturday would be our biggest day. I wanted to prepare the shop today, especially if I received another call from Momo. I checked in with her last night, and she said she and Nora were fine as could be. In between work I'd call her again, as I was worried about her. She had taken on a lot by having Nora move in with her, and now Paige's death added another element she hadn't expected to deal with.

Nubi and I left my apartment and found his friends waiting for him.

"Good morning, Cleopatra and Nefertiti. Have you been waiting long for Nubi?" I followed Nubi to his friends, who sat still as statues four feet away from my door. Their bright eyes had an intensity as strong as their human mother, Ruby Virtue. Were they psychic like her? I've heard of pet psychics who communicate with animals but not the other way around.If there were cat psychics, they would definitely be found here in the French Quarter.

I turned my head to the sound of Ruby's door opening. I

steeled myself, waiting for a snarky comment from Ruby, but she wasn't the one leaving the apartment.

"Good morning, Papa."

Dressed in a wrinkled white tunic shirt and matching pants, he jumped like a college boy being caught leaving the girls' dormitory. His python-topped cane almost fell from his hand, but he caught it in time.

"Good morning, Sammy. You sure did scare me." Papa walked over and kissed me on the cheek. "But it's sure nice to see your beautiful smile this morning."

"It's good to see your handsome smile this morning. I didn't mean to startle you."

"Now, you just wipe that grin off your face. Ruby and I watched a late movie, so I slept on her couch." Papa took out his handkerchief and patted down his bald head.

I held back my laughter. Papa, despite his age, still cared about appearances. "I've heard that excuse before. You and Ruby are grown-ups, remember? You're allowed to have sleepovers with no one questioning your virtue."

"I'll remember that." His laughter caught the attention of all three cats, who slinked over to rub up against Papa's legs. "My goodness, you cats are going to mess up my good pants."

"I don't think you care by the way you're scratching their heads," I said.

"Shhh, don't tell them that. Next, they'll think they can play with my cane and what will I do then?" When I first met Papa, he leaned on the cane to walk, but since he had renewed his friendship with Ruby, he appeared to only carry the cane as an accessory.

"Your secret is safe with me." I tried to hide a yawn, but Papa saw it.

"Honey, you must be exhausted after yesterday's disturbance. That poor child. No one should die so young." Papa shook his head.

"I agree. It's heartbreaking for Paige's family and friends."

"It certainly is. But let's talk of happy things. Are you excited about your birthday? Ruby and I are looking forward to your party." Papa started toward the courtyard gate and I followed him.

"Ruby is coming, too?" My cranky next-door neighbor had been less cranky since spending more time with Papa, but she still liked to throw her insults at me. Although she hasn't called me "trouble" lately, so I guess that was progress.

"Of course! She wants to be there." Papa held the courtyard gate open for me. "Ruby may seem uninterested, but she does care about everyone here at Thibodeaux Mansion."

"I'm glad to hear it," I said.

"Are you heading to work? Do you have time for beignets and café au lait?" Papa gently placed his hand on my shoulder. "You appear to have a lot on your mind. I have two good ears."

"Oh, I'm fine." I would have loved to go with Papa. Our chats over our favorite food were some of my favorites. He loved telling stories of his childhood in New Orleans, and I couldn't get enough of them. I really wished he would write a book, as I hated the thought of his history being forgotten.

"I have to get to the shop, but thanks for asking."

"I'll just take a rain check, Sammy. I'm here if you need me. Remember that." Papa squeezed my shoulder and headed down Royal Street in the other direction.

I don't think I will ever get tired of walking through the French Quarter. Although I walk the same street every time

I go to Lagniappe Books, I notice different things each time. Last week, beautiful dripping ferns filled the top floor of a town house that had been empty before. Occasionally a new artist would pop up in front of St. Anthony's Garden with a unique paint style all of their own. There was always music in the air, but it could vary from a four-piece band to a single singer. Today there was a woman sitting in front of a typewriter offering to write a poem on the spot. New Orleans had so many creative people, and I loved all of it.

As soon as I arrived at the shop, I had two surprise visitors.

"Hey, Sammy! We figured you and Andrew could use some breakfast this morning." Neal Bennett raised a paper bag with one hand and pulled me in for a hug with the other. No matter the weather, Neal wore cargo shorts and a New Orleans Past & Present Tours T-shirt. When I first met him, he came across as a goofy skateboarding twenty-something. He still does, but he's also the owner of his own tour company and a true friend to everyone.

"If you brought sweet potato scones from Libby, I'll love you even more." I accepted the bag from Neal and opened it. The intoxicating smell of sweet potato and cinnamon filled the air. The scones came from Libby Tyler's café, Artistic Coffee & Creations. She baked the best scones in the world in addition to being the co-owner of Thibodeaux Mansion and the mother of my boyfriend.

"I don't think that's possible, Sammy. Or at least don't tell Connor that." Neal brushed his long brown bangs out of his eyes. "Or Nubi."

"Ha, ha! We all know Rose loves you the most. Right, Jasper?" I laughed.

"I agree, but I wouldn't say otherwise. I want Rose to let me into The Gas Light." Jasper St. Martin handed me a cup of coffee. My cousin wore jeans and a New Orleans Past & Present T-shirt, so he must be working with Neal today. His over-six-foot-tall body appeared relaxed today, which wasn't usually the case the day after his mother arrived in town. He loved her dearly, but as much as she tried, Aunt Charlene couldn't always help but smother him often.

"Have you seen your mom yet?" I asked him.

"I've talked to her, but I haven't actually seen her. She spent the evening with Momo and her friend." Jasper grinned. "She and Momo have hit it off, apparently."

"Your mom was a huge help with Momo's friend Nora. Especially after the news about their friend," I said.

"Sorry, I should have asked how you were doing." Jasper hugged me.

"Yeah, sorry. Have they said it was murder? And by *they*, I mean, Rob and Christine, not Winston." Neal rolled his eyes. Winston irritated just about everyone in the French Quarter. How he still found information was beyond me.

"Not that I've heard." I shook my head. "But do either one of you know Tate King? He was Paige's boyfriend."

"I've heard of him, but Rose knows him. She kicked him out of The Gas Light last year," Neal said.

"Whoa! What did he do? I've never seen Rose make anyone leave," Jasper said.

I hadn't either. As the bartender at our local bar, The Gas Light, Rose ran a tight ship. Through a steely gaze or a firm, "Cut it out!" anyone trying to cause trouble stopped. Apparently Tate was the exception.

"He was angry after she cut him off and wouldn't stop bothering other people. When he tried to go behind the bar to serve himself, Rose threw him out," Neal said.

"Literally?" I asked.

"She could have, but Tate slinked out on his own after

the whole bar yelled at him. No one bothers Rose at The Gas Light." Neal smiled. As Rose's boyfriend, Neal took pride in any and everything she did. The feeling was mutual with Rose.

"Do you know if he found another bar to go to?" I asked.

"You should ask Rose. Bartenders share stories and the names of customers who cause trouble," Neal said. "Do you think Tate killed Paige?"

"I don't know, but I'd love to hear his side of the story. Assuming Rob and Christine haven't arrested him. The family definitely didn't like him," I said.

"But that doesn't make him a killer," Jasper said. "If you go see him, take someone with you, okay?"

"I promise," I said. "Thanks again for the coffee and scones. I'll see y'all later?" I said.

"Definitely. We're off to see Mama now," Jasper said.

"Wish us luck. She said she has more birthday party work for us to do." Neal grinned.

"Remember, no karaoke machines!" I yelled as Neal and Jasper left me on the stoop of Lagniappe Books.

They both laughed loudly before heading down the street. Did they know something I didn't know about the party? I better talk to Aunt Charlene today and make sure she hasn't come up some other over-the-top party idea. I'd had enough surprises for the week.

12

Work was uneventful, which I appreciated. The steady flow of customers kept my mind off of Paige's death. I did take a quick break in the late morning to call Momo. I offered to come over after work, but Momo said it wasn't necessary. "We're just taking it slow today," she said. "Nora regrets not going to see Lydia and Dorothy, but she did talk to them briefly last night. They're still in shock, poor things."

"Would you like to join Beau and me for dinner? We're going to the Garden District tonight. I know you love Gris-Gris," Andrew asked as he locked the shop's door at 6 p.m.

I did love that restaurant. Sitting upstairs on the balcony with a bowl of luscious chicken and dumplings was wonderful. Taking in the view of the shops along Magazine street was a lovely experience. I wondered if the residents who lived above the shops watched the diners liked we watched them. I never said no to an invitation there, but tonight I had other plans.

"Sissy and I are having a movie night, otherwise I would

totally join you two," I said. "I feel like I haven't seen Beau in ages, though."

Beau Boudreaux was busy preparing Hotel Jeanne for the upcoming holidays. His savvy business sense made him successful in all his businesses, but the hotel industry was still new to him. This being his first holiday season, he was working constantly to make it the finest one the hotel ever had.

"He finally agreed to take a night off. Ambrose thanked me for taking him out to dinner." Andrew chuckled. "I don't think Ambrose has quite adjusted fully to Beau's exuberance."

Beau inherited Ambrose Fortner as the manager when he bought Hotel Jeanne. After a rocky start they had settled into a good working relationship. "Nothing could have prepared him for all the Christmas trees Beau wants."

"I know. Wait until you see all the trees he has set up in his home." Andrew laughed. "Have a good night with Sissy. I'll see you in the morning."

We parted ways, and I headed back to Thibodeaux Mansion. I wasn't the only resident going home. Although I could only see her from the back, I recognized the long silk purple dress and the matching scarf holding back silver hair. I quickened my pace and began walking next to her.

"Hi, Ruby."

"It took you long enough to realize it was me. I felt your presence two blocks ago." Ruby turned to face me with a frown. "You have spirits surrounding you. What trouble have you caused today?"

I generally tried to ignore Ruby's insults, but tonight was not the night. "I have not caused any trouble. Perhaps the spirits are around me since I unfortunately discovered a dead young woman yesterday."

"Oh." She turned a slight shade of red. "Was it Paige Townsend?"

"Did you know her?" I couldn't imagine how the two women would have crossed paths. But then again, more people went to psychics and tarot card readers more than people realized, I imagined. Especially here in New Orleans.

"I only met her once at a fundraiser her mother hosted. I normally don't attend those types of functions, but this was for cats," Ruby said. "Paige had a bright pink aura, so I knew she was kind and caring. When she told me she was a nurse it made sense."

"Are you friends, then, with her mother, Lydia?"

Ruby looked at me as if I had asked her if she had three legs. "We don't run in the same circles as you might have guessed. She tried to get me to join another one of her charities, but I don't support eradicating the fire ants in the city. Let the insects be."

Obviously Ruby had never been bitten by a fire ant. As a child in Florida, I ran into a mound of them. Every mother at the playground helped bat them off me. The pain from the bites eventually went away, but I still have a scar on my ankle from the biggest and meanest ant.

"Do you know her sister, Dorothy Merritt?" I said.

"I met her that same night. She treated me like fresh meat." Ruby shook her head, making her dangling silver bead earrings swing like chandeliers.

"F-fresh meat?" I stammered. "As in you were a new potential donor to the cat charity?"

"Not for the charity. I don't think she cared about it. Once she found out I had a daughter, she wanted to know all about her. As soon as I told her we were estranged, Dorothy left me. Later, I learned she was trying to find a suitable match for her son."

"That conversation must have been years ago since you and Verity are talking once again," I said. "Not that you would have wanted her to date Emerson Merritt, I imagine."

Ruby pressed her lips together, but I could see a small smile forming. While she and Verity weren't close, they were working on it. Verity and I were friends now, and she kept me up to date on their progress. I hoped she would visit New Orleans soon, not just for Ruby but for all of us at Thibodeaux Mansion. She had fit right in when she came back to town.

"Exactly. Even if I felt he was suitable for Verity, I doubt she or any woman would be good enough, in Dorothy's eyes. Any time I see her out with her son, it's apparent she thinks he walks on water."

I laughed. "Doesn't every parent believe their child can do no wrong?"

"No, we all do not. In my case, I love my child and appreciate her gifts, but she is not without fault." Ruby sighed. "But our faults should not define us."

Normally I would have come back with some snarky remark, but not now. Ruby rarely shared anything about herself so I wouldn't ruin this moment. And I didn't need to argue with her. I agreed with her for once.

We kept walking and passed by a restaurant I hadn't been to yet.

"Have you eaten here, Ruby?" I asked as we passed the Vampire Café. While the restaurant and gift shop seemed to cater to tourists, it was known for its good food and interesting merchandise. Papa had mentioned to me that he and Ruby were trying different restaurants in the Quarter.

"No." Ruby's wrinkles deepened as she frowned.

"Why not? Don't you think real vampires visit the restaurant?" I laughed.

"Real vampires aren't going to go to a café and then go shopping afterward. Really, Samantha, you shouldn't believe everything you see."

Ruby picked up the pace before I could ask her if she actually believed in vampires. When it came to the supernatural world, I never knew if she was joking or being serious. The one thing I did know she was being serious about was Lydia and Dorothy. While they might have their faults, as Ruby said, our faults don't define us. But could they be the reason for Paige's death?

13

Ruby and I entered the courtyard to find Aunt Charlene and Nora waiting for me.

"There you are, Sammy and Miss Ruby, too! I knocked on both of your doors, but didn't imagine y'all were out together." Aunt Charlene bounded out of the chair next to my front door.

Ruby looked like a deer caught in headlights, not knowing if she should stay still or run away. Aunt Charlene gravitated to Ruby every time she came to visit. Her boisterous nature was the opposite to Ruby's quiet reserve. Knowing Aunt Charlene, she thought she could get Ruby to loosen up. So far, it hadn't worked.

"We were not out together. Samantha caught up with me as we both walked home," Ruby said.

"Well, I'm glad y'all walked in together. I wanted to ask if you would do your thing for Sammy's birthday party," Charlene said.

"My thing?" Ruby raised her eyebrows.

"Your tarot card reading, silly!" Charlene playfully swatted Ruby's arm. "Ooh, maybe a seance, too?"

Ruby's pinched expression relayed her feelings clearly, but she said, "No."

"But..." Aunt Charlene's face dropped like a child who had lost her balloon. I prayed she wouldn't flop on the floor and throw a tantrum.

"Hello. I am Ruby Virtue. Are you a friend of Samantha's and Charlene's?" Ruby crossed over to Nora. She sat still in her wheelchair, but she grinned as she watched Ruby and Charlene's interaction.

"I'm Nora Winslow. I am their friend, but also Momo's." Nora reached out her hand. "She's told me all about you. Not just the bad, I promise."

I stifled a laugh, as I assumed Ruby wouldn't appreciate it. But to my surprise, she chuckled. "I wouldn't expect anything less from Momo. We have our differences, but I believe we understand one another more as the years go by."

Momo and Ruby's estrangement began decades ago, after Momo's niece and Ruby's daughter disappeared. The revelations that followed the reappearance of them brought Momo and Ruby together. No one would refer to them as best friends, but I had spied them having drinks together on Momo's balcony.

"Time passing has a way of revealing things we never imagined." Nora shivered, and pulled up the blanket that had slid off her knees.

"Yes, it does. I hope this will not upset you, but you have spirits watching you from afar." Ruby pointed toward the back of the courtyard where the water fountain turned planter sat.

"You mean the cats?" I blurted out. Sometimes I can't help myself when Ruby refers to spirits around the courtyard.

"No." Ruby's glare spoke volumes. "I can't quite make them out, but it appears to be an older couple and a young man. I've tried to get them to come closer so I may speak with them, but they appear to be apprehensive."

My face grew warm when Nora stretched her neck as if she was looking for the spirits. "Have they said anything at all? Ask them if they're Simon and Cathy Winslow and Hollis Davenport."

"I'm sorry, but they have left." Ruby placed her hand on Nora's. "I'm sure they will come to you when the time is right."

With that, Ruby gave me one last dirty look and unlocked her door. Aunt Charlene said, "Ruby, come on out here and stay with us. We have an extra hurricane if you'd like."

Sure enough, there were three large white plastic cups from Pat O'Brien's. Two of them were half-empty, but the other was to the brim and with the orange and cherry garnish still intact.

"No, thank you, Charlene. Have a good evening." Ruby smiled at my aunt and then Nora. Well, at least she liked them.

"To what do I owe the pleasure of your visit this evening?" I asked.

"We brought you a hurricane. I know you like Pimm's Cups, but Nora wanted to go to Pat O'Brien's," Aunt Charlene answered.

"Yes, one last hurrah there." Nora reached for the cup and took a sip. "We were quite the sight, us two old ladies drinking hurricanes."

"Should you be drinking, Nora?" I kept my voice calm, hoping my concern wouldn't come through.

"I only take the heavy stuff at night, so don't you worry. But I might not need it tonight." Nora laughed.

I stepped in front of Aunt Charlene so Nora couldn't hear me. "Do you think it was a good idea to let Nora drink?"

"I told the bartender to add a little bit of rum just so she could taste it," Charlene whispered. "I had him do it for all three. Nora wanted to go there because she and Hollis used to go there for the hurricanes. But I also think she needed to forget about Paige's death for a bit."

"Oh. That was kind and smart of you." I let out a sigh of relief, but I felt guilty. Aunt Charlene handled the situation beautifully, and I shouldn't have jumped to conclusions.

"Thank you, darling." Aunt Charlene patted my cheek gently.

"I assumed the third drink is for Momo. Where is she?" I said.

"She went out to a poker game with her friends. I had no idea Momo played poker like I do," Aunt Charlene said. "We're going to teach Nora how to play, tomorrow."

The creak of the courtyard gate opening interrupted our moment. Sissy sauntered into the courtyard, carrying two bags.

"Aunt Charlene. I wondered when I'd get to see you!" Sissy dropped her bags and hugged my aunt. "I brought home gumbo and a stack of wedding magazines from my momma."

"Now that's the perfect combination!" Aunt Charlene clapped her hands. "Nora, have you met Sissy? She's the sweetest thing."

"Thank you. I think the same of you." Sissy smiled. "It's nice to meet you, Miss Nora. I know Momo is so happy to have you staying with her."

Nora accepted Sissy's handshake. "Momo speaks very highly of you."

"I would love to hear your stories about Momo. Unless she's sworn you to secrecy," Sissy said.

"If you share your gumbo, I might be persuaded to tell a story or two." Nora's laughter illuminated her face.

"It's a deal." Sissy returned to her bags and picked them up. "Should we eat inside your place, Sammy?"

I unlocked my door and let Sissy inside to set up dinner. Rob joked my apartment was Sissy's second home. She treated it like her own, especially when she brought home-cooked meals from her mother, who lived in Metairie. I joked she only brought food to share because she wanted to hang out with Nubi. Sissy claimed not to be a cat person, but she snuck him treats whenever she saw him.

"Let me get you inside, Nora. Would you like me to push you in, or would you like to walk?" Aunt Charlene said.

"I'd like to sit outside for a moment, and then I can walk inside. My hurricane hasn't gone to my head." Nora took another sip of her drink. "Sammy, will you join me out here?"

"Of course." I took the seat across from Nora.

"I'll go and help Sissy," Aunt Charlene said. "Sissy, let me see those bridal magazines. We still need to talk about your wedding colors."

Even though Sissy's mother had taken the lead in the wedding plans, Sissy included Aunt Charlene. Sissy claimed my aunt's knowledge of flowers was a big help. I knew she included her for another reason. My cousin Scarlett's death left a huge hole in her life, especially when it came to those milestones Scarlett would never reach.

Nubi slipped out of the apartment before the door closed. He meowed at me either in greeting or to complain

I'd left him too long. He ignored me and jumped into Nora's lap. She laughed as Nubi sniffed her chin, put his front paws on Nora's shoulders, and sniffed the rest of her face. I'd never seen Nubi do this before.

"What a gorgeous cat. This must be the famous Anubis, or rather Nubi." Nora stroked Nubi's belly after he curled up on her lap.

"Yes, that's him. Did Momo tell you about him?"

"She did, and she told me the story. Well, the parts you told her. I imagine you kept somethings to yourself," Nora said.

"Don't we all?" I smiled at Nora.

"Touché, my dear." Nora winked. "But tell me how you ended up here in New Orleans."

I started with the short version, telling Nora how I was found abandoned after Hurricane Geoffrey and adopted by the Richardsons. Nora listened intently as I explained how I moved here to find out about my past after my parents died in a car crash. While it led to Thibodeaux Mansion and my newfound family, my move here brought out the worst in my brother. The murders that followed, along with his death, were more than I could bear at times. But my family, both found and biological, kept me here.

"So you ran to your past while I ran away from mine. I'm impressed with you, Sammy." Nora tilted her head to the side. "You are stronger than I ever was at your age."

"But you did come back to visit, didn't you?"

"I did every few years, but I didn't go back to Hollis's house. I'd meet his sisters at a restaurant. I just couldn't face returning to where he died. Our last moments in that court-yard were filled with anger and frustration."

"I'm so sorry." There was an ache in my throat as I listened to Nora.

"Thank you. I surprised myself by accepting Momo's offer to stay here. New Orleans holds the best and worst memories for me. I hoped the good times would outweigh the horrible ones in my mind. But with Hollis's note and now Paige's death, I'm not so sure."

New Orleans also held the best and worst memories for me, too. At times, the worst overpowered the best, but it didn't last for long. I didn't want to define my life by the bad things that had happened. It seems like Nora was trying to do the same. But the past and the present weren't letting her.

"Nora, I hope you won't mind if I ask you about the card from Hollis. What about it made you say you shouldn't have killed him?" I asked gently.

"I finally talked to Momo about it last night, so I guess it's your turn."

"Sorry, I didn't mean to offend you," I said.

Nora shook her head. "No, I'm not offended. I just can't believe I said what I've been thinking for the past years out loud. And in front of Hollis's family."

"You really think you killed him?" I placed my hand on Nora's trembling hand.

"I hope not," she whispered.

I thought the same thing. But I needed to hear her story to make a decision.

14

———

I gave Nora a moment to collect herself. Although Thibodeaux Mansion was on a busy street, the court-yard was quiet most of the time. If a loud group of people walked by the gate, their voices would come through. I'd learned to block it out most of the time.

But I never did that with the music that drifted in from our neighbors. Lately, a clarinetist played deep soulful music in the late afternoon. Since all our courtyards had tall walls, I hadn't seen who the musician was. I'd told Sissy that we should grab a ladder to meet the mystery musician. She had laughed and said, "Honey, people already call you nosy, so that might be a bit much." I hated to say but I agreed with her.

Tonight there was no music, no cats rustling in the plants in the old water fountain, and no voices. All I heard was Nora breathing deeply and then exhaling long breaths. When her breathing returned to normal I said, "Why don't you tell me what happened that night?"

Nora began her story. "Hollis and I headed over to Brennan's to celebrate my birthday. We had such a lovely meal. I

85

had turtle soup and Bananas Foster for the first and only time. Have you been there?"

I didn't want to push Nora too fast in telling her story, but I didn't want to get offtrack. Instead of answering out loud, I just shook my head.

"So we had an incredible meal with too much wine and then stopped off for a nightcap at Pat O'Brien's." Nora twirled the straw in her hurricane cup. "I begged him to give me my presents at the bar, but he said they were back home. He also promised my answer would be there."

Feeling tipsy and annoyed that they had to go to his house for her gifts, Nora admitted she was in a foul mood when they entered the courtyard. "I waited by the fountain while Emerson ran into the guesthouse to get my gifts. Dorothy and Lydia both came out to wish me a happy birthday. I tried to put on a happy face, but the effects of the drinks made it difficult."

"Did they both live there, too?"

"Dorothy did with her late husband and Emerson, who was just a boy. Lydia was staying there at night because her late husband was out of town, and Paige was a colicky baby. Dorothy was a big help, apparently," Nora said.

"So you saw the sisters that night?"

"Just for a bit. Once Hollis came out with a present, he shooed them away." Nora gave a slight smile. "They weren't happy, to say the least. Dorothy insisted they should stay, since she helped pick out my gift. Lydia finally convinced Dorothy to leave us alone."

Looking back, Nora realized the sisters wanted to hear what Hollis had to say about joining the peace corps with her. They had been asking her if she still planned to leave after the fall semester and if Hollis was joining her. She told them repeatedly, she didn't know.

"By the time they finally went back into the main house, I was thoroughly annoyed and definitely drunk." Tears meandered down Nora's face. "I yelled at Hollis that he needed to just tell me if he was going or not. And that he better tell his sisters right after because I couldn't take their constant pestering."

Hollis became annoyed and was undeniably drunk by this time, too. He shoved the present in my hands and yelled, "Just open the card, Nora. You're ruining the mood."

"I can't imagine you took that well." I gave one of the bar napkins to her to dry her eyes.

"You're right. I opened my gift, which was obviously a book, by the shape of it. My behavior was childish. I didn't even open the card. Instead, I shoved it in the book where it stayed until you found it two days ago."

A breeze blew through the courtyard, making both of us shudder. Even Nubi raised his head and sniffed the air. He curled back up in Nora's lap as she petted him. Nora's tears subsided, and she continued remembering that night.

"Hollis told me I wouldn't find out if he was coming with me until I read the card and found my second gift. By this time, I'd had enough and told him, 'If you can't just tell me, you must not be coming with me.' He wasn't happy with me."

They continued arguing for a few more minutes until Nora decided to leave. "We really were arguing over nothing, but I just wanted him to give me a straight answer. He loved joking around, but I'd had enough. I stomped toward the courtyard gate but tripped over my own feet. Hollis picked me up off the ground and twirled me around."

Nora became nauseous and angry as Hollis tried to talk to her. When he finally put her down, she pushed him with all her might. "I know I don't look it now, but I was built pretty solid back then. Hollis fell backward onto the ground. I grabbed the book and headed toward the gate."

"Did he fall into the water fountain?" I had a hard time believing Hollis died from a fall backwards. The surrounding bricks of the water fountain seemed a more likely place to cause bodily damage.

"Funny you ask. Paige asked me the same thing," Nora said. "He landed about fifteen feet away from it. When I left, he was lying on the ground yelling for me to come back."

Nora glanced away and squeezed her hands. "He was alive when I left, but for all these years, I worried I pushed him so hard that he cracked his head. I've lived with the thought that my stupidity and anger caused his death."

Sobs wracked Nora's body as she cried. Aunt Charlene poked her head out from my apartment door. I mouthed, "She's fine." My aunt nodded and went back inside. I handed Nora napkins until her tears subsided.

"I'm so sorry, Sammy. You don't need to be out here consoling a stupid old woman." Nora smiled weakly.

"I'm glad to be here for you, Nora. This must have been hard to have on your mind for all this time."

"It has, and now it's even worse learning that Hollis was going to leave with me. We could have had a whole life together if I hadn't..." Nora bit her lip.

"Nora, it's not your fault," I said. "What did the police say about Hollis's death?"

"Dorothy told me the police said he died from a head wound." Nora turned red. "I didn't stay after the funeral. My parents came and got me a few days later. I joined the peace corps a month later."

"Did you speak to the police before you left?" I asked.

"Yes. I told them what I told you. Hollis's parents weren't thrilled, to say the least."

"I assume they didn't want to hear about Hollis being drunk," I said.

"You're right. I didn't blame them, but at least they didn't blame me for his death. At least to me or his sisters. Dorothy told me that the family had decided that Hollis's death was a tragic accident."

"And the police must have thought the same, but you didn't?"

Nora shook her head. "Would he have fallen if we hadn't fought? If I had just opened the card, I would have known he was coming with me and the night would have been completely different."

Nubi meowed, whether in agreement or to console Nora, I didn't know. But he brought solace to Nora.

"I wish I had adopted a cat. They really are amazing beings." Nora scratched the little white spot of fur on Nubi's head.

"I agree. Nubi brings me comfort all the time," I said. "Thank you for sharing your story with me. If my opinion means anything, I don't think you killed him. I agree with Hollis's parents; it was a tragic accident."

"I appreciate that, Sammy. Really, I do. But I wish I could know definitely what really happened to Hollis." Nora looked me straight in the eyes. "Momo and Charlene both said you're good at solving mysteries. Maybe you can solve this one."

Nora didn't add "before I die," but the sentiment came through loud and clear. How could I say no?

"I'll do my best, Nora. But I can't promise you I'll find the answer for you," I said.

"That's all I can ask." Nora reached over Nubi and grasped my hand. "Actually, there is one more thing. Could you look into Paige's death, too?"

"Of course. I'll try."

It wasn't as if I hadn't been asking already about her death. But again, I didn't want to promise I would have answers for Nora before she passed on. I would try my hardest, though. While Nora was a new friend to me, I meant to do my best to give her some solace.

My head ached at the thought of how this could go wrong. I didn't want Nora dying without knowing the truth. But what if she killed Hollis? Did I want her going to her grave with that horrible news?

15

Nora and I joined Aunt Charlene and Sissy in my apartment for dinner. Nora yawned throughout the meal. She apologized each time: "I'm sorry. That hurricane made me sleepy. I can't handle my liquor like I used to."

Aunt Charlene and I exchanged smiles, knowing there was barely any rum in the drinks, although there was no denying Nora's exhaustion. The rest of us finished our gumbo quickly. Sissy offered to walk the ladies to Momo's house with my help.

"I'm not saying you can't get Miss Nora home on your own." Sissy put her arm around an indignant Aunt Charlene. "But I know where all the potholes and cracked sidewalks are, so we'll get there quickly."

"Well, if you insist. Thank you, darling." Aunt Charlene's face relaxed. She had been yawning during dinner, too, so I hadn't expected her to protest too much.

The gaslights lit the way to Momo's house. There's a different energy to the French Quarter at night. Nothing is more true over on Bourbon Street with its neon signs, loud music, people dancing in the street, and the occasional throwing of beads off balconies even when it wasn't Mardi Gras. When tourists ask me about Bourbon Street, I recommend going there at least once to take in the festive atmosphere, But if they aren't fans of never ending loud parties, I suggest they try Frenchmen Street in the Marigny. The street is lined with restaurants and bars, many of them offering live music every night. I preferred to go there, especially if Connor was playing at the bar, Note by Note.

But the rest of the French Quarter differs from Bourbon Street. Restaurants were filled with tourists and locals alike enjoying Cajun and Creole food. With full bellies, they'd wander the streets in the darkness searching for music, shopping, a bar, or sometimes just their hotel.

We walked Aunt Charlene and Nora slowly back to Momo's house. Watching Nora take in the sights and sounds of the French Quarter made me smile. She swayed to the music from a trumpet player performing on a street corner and insisted on tipping him twenty dollars. When we passed Anthony's Garden at the back of St. Louis Cathedral, Nora demanded we stop.

"Hollis and I always did this when we passed by." Nora raised her arms like she was signaling a touchdown. We all joined her and then I had to explain to a few curious passerby what we were doing. The Sacred Heart of Jesus statue was nicknamed Touchdown Jesus as the shadow it cast at night made it appear he was signaling a touch down. Some of the onlookers did it along with us for a second time.

Nora's demeanor changed from joy to sadness from time to time. Most of the time she smiled, but every now and then, her shoulders would slump. Just before we reached the house, a young couple beaming at each other walked by us. A tear slipped out as we reached Momo's house. Sissy handed Nora a tissue and she wiped her eyes quickly.

"Let me get the door, and then I'll help you inside, Nora." Aunt Charlene took a single key out of her purse.

"Momo gave you a key?" I said.

"Of course she did. How am I supposed to get in when she's not home?" Aunt Charlene gave me a puzzled look. "Oh, didn't I tell you? I'm staying here with Momo and Nora."

"No, you didn't." Now I was even more worried about Momo's stress levels. Aunt Charlene had proven helpful with Nora, but adding another person to her household surely would be stressful, won't it?

"Charlene is such a big help." Nora smiled at my aunt. "Not just with me, but she's helping Momo clean and organize the house. She's such a breath of fresh air for us."

"Oh, hush. You're making me blush." Charlene laughed.

"I'm sure she's a great addition to the house. But let me help you inside. I need to practice my nursing skills, or Aunt Charlene will take my job at the hospital." Sissy grinned and offered her arm to Nora. Before they stepped inside, Sissy turned and winked at me. I was so lucky to have a best friend who could read my mind.

After they were halfway down the hall, I asked, "Aunt Charlene, that's very kind of you to help them out. I assume that's why you're staying here."

"You're worried Beau kicked me out, aren't you?" Aunt Charlene planted her hands on her hips.

"No..."

"Honey, I'm just kidding!" Charlene hugged me. "Beau says I always have a place at his hotel. And not just because what happened to my baby girl."

Beau had offered my aunt unlimited stays at his hotel.

People who didn't know Beau assumed he did it so my aunt wouldn't sue him for her daughter's death in the hotel pool. But it wasn't Beau's style to do something like that. He truly felt horrible about Scarlett's death and wanted Aunt Charlene to visit as often as she liked. "I feel close to her when I sit by the pool. Her spirit is here, not at the cemetery back home," Charlene said to Beau. That's all he needed to keep a room open for her at all times.

"I know. Beau adores you. We all do." That was the truth. Aunt Charlene was part of the Thibodeaux Mansion family. We'd all come to love her and realize that her over-the-top personality was just part of who she was. Although, it wasn't always easy to take.

"And I love all of y'all." Aunt Charlene's smile lit up her face. "Momo actually asked me to help with Nora as long as I can stay. She offered a bedroom, so I said yes."

"Thank you for helping Momo," I said.

"Of course! We old Southern ladies have to stick together."

"You're not as old as Momo, but you two are Southern, through and through." I laughed.

Sissy came out of the house and put her arm around Aunt Charlene's shoulder. "Nora really appreciates you're staying with them. Not just for her, but for Momo also. She's worried that Momo has taken on too much."

"Momo won't admit it, but she's slowing down a bit." Aunt Charlene sighed. "Now, she takes pride in doing everything on her own, but sometimes you have to ask for help."

Sissy gave me a pointed look. When I first moved here, I didn't ask for help, and I found myself in a deadly situation. I learned to ask for help...most of the time.

"Very true. Nora is in bed, and I expect she'll be asleep before you go see her. She's exhausted, but she had a wonderful evening. Thanks to you, Aunt Charlene," Sissy said.

"Thanks, darling. We all made the night special for her." Aunt Charlene kissed us both on the cheek. "I'll go check on Nora and then take my shoes off. It's been a long day."

Aunt Charlene waved goodbye as she entered the house. I was just about to ask Sissy if we should pick up some ice cream and watch a movie when she grabbed my arm.

"Look, Gideon's having another party." Sure enough, Gideon was on his doorstep waving goodbye to a couple. Loud music escaped from the house until he closed the door behind him. Smart move, as the neighbors, including Momo and Beau, have complained about the noise.

"Sorry, Sissy, but we need to go to that party." I hopped down the stairs.

"Excuse me? You never want to go to any of his parties. Do have the sudden need to buy art? Granted, it's for charity..."

"No, I don't. The man Gideon Pearce is welcoming inside is Emerson Merritt. This is my chance to talk to him. Are you in?"

"Aren't I always?" Sissy threaded her arm through mine. We headed toward Gideon's house to hopefully find more answers about Paige's death.

16

***

Sissy and I walked into Gideon's house and stopped in horror. From the outside, the home appeared to be a traditional French Quarter town house. Painted in soft peach with bright teal shutters with a wrought-iron balcony across the second, the home fit in to the neighborhood perfectly.

The same couldn't be said about the inside. Anything from its original build was gone. The inside had been gutted. All the walls were white, and the floor was polished concrete. If Gideon was going for the modern-art-gallery-with-no-soul image, he nailed it.

At least the art brought life to the rooms. The paintings on the walls varied from brightly colored, splashy abstracts to muted oil paintings of detailed New Orleans' landmarks. I spotted a bronze sculpture that looked like the one Momo described the other night. However, the haphazard edges on each side suggested that the boat was rushed to be split in half. So that must be how they got the sculpture inside. Momo would cackle in her bourbon when I told her about this.

But it was a shame to take all that history out of a home. I understand things need to be modernized, but to strip out all the history and character was too much. One of the many reasons I loved New Orleans was for the respect and preservation of the architecture. Sissy felt the same way.

In my ear, she whispered, "They should arrest Gideon for what he's done to this house."

"I agree, but then again, are you surprised? The man dresses like Mark Twain going to a disco." Whether or not it was on purpose, Gideon styled his white hair and mustache in the style of Mark Twain. But his choice of bright, shiny suits at least a size too small made him look anything like an old Southern gentleman.

Sissy giggled. "You've got that right. Okay, let's go find Emerson. I don't want to stay here any longer than necessary. We might make it out of here before Gideon sees us."

"Sounds like a plan. We'll be here all night if Gideon sees we finally took him up on his offer to see his house."

Sissy took two champagne glasses from a passing server. "Here, take a glass. We'll fit in more if we look like we're here for the party and not to interrogate a potential murder suspect."

"You're really paying attention to all the mystery shows we're watching." I raised my eyebrows. "Or is Rob giving you pointers?"

"Ha! He gets to show a badge to get people to talk." Sissy took a sip and wrinkled her nose. "Ugh, this has got to be cheap champagne or a bad year. But seriously, we need to be casual or we'll scare him off."

We walked through the living and dining rooms, admiring the artwork. We ran into a few acquaintances, so we stopped here and there to chat. Once we left the courtyard, we found our target.

In the back of the courtyard, Emerson stood by a bronze statue of an enormous catfish on the far side of the pool. He was speaking with an older couple. Sissy and I strolled through the area, trying to make our approach to Emerson seem casual. We stopped a few feet away, admiring another statue and eavesdropping.

"Yes, I will let my mother and aunt know you send your sympathies. I'm sure they will appreciate it." Emerson shook the man's hand and kissed the woman on the cheek. "Now, remember to call me when you're ready to switch over to my new bank. It'll be great to work with y'all again."

The couple mumbled their goodbyes and beelined toward the server with a tray of champagne. By the side glances they gave each other, I guessed their conversation with Emerson puzzled them. I was puzzled, too. Who talks business in the same breath as giving thanks for sympathies for your deceased cousin?

"Hello, Emerson. I'm Samantha..."

"Yes, of course." Emerson leaned down and kissed me on the cheek. "I hope you have recovered from the shock of yesterday. Thank goodness you were there for Aunt Lydia."

I froze for a moment, as I didn't expect him to be so friendly or to kiss me. "I'm fine, but how are your aunt and your mom? And how are you?"

"We're all as good as we can be. I'm not sure how we'll get over Paige's death." Emerson shook his head solemnly. "Have you heard anything from the police? I hope they've found Paige's ex-boyfriend. If it wasn't an accident, it must have been him."

"I haven't heard anything. So you think her ex-boyfriend is responsible for her death?" I asked.

"Tate King was no good for Paige. He was dragging Paige down along with him."

"Why do you say that?" I said.

"He had his addictions and money problems. Paige could only help him so much. She was too kind and it might have killed her." Emerson waved over a server and swapped his empty champagne glass for a fresh one.

Sissy and I gave each other the *Can you believe this?* glance. From what we had heard, Paige and Tate both had addiction problems, although it appeared Paige had worked through them. But it was obvious that Emerson had nothing good to say about Tate. Hopefully, we'd hear something from Rob about him.

"But let's not talk of tragedy. Although it's hard for me to leave my family, Aunt Lydia insisted I come tonight. She and Gideon are co-chairs of the upcoming arts gala, so she felt the family should be represented at all the events." Emerson puffed out his chest.

Once again, Sissy and I gave each other the glance. Somehow, having a family representative at a party for a charity didn't seem like a priority. Or was that just an excuse for Emerson to show up tonight?

"I'm sorry I haven't introduced myself. I'm Emerson Merritt. You must be a friend of Samantha's." Emerson reached out to shake Sissy's hand. "Have we met before? You seem familiar. Did we meet at the White Linen party this summer? I'm sure I wouldn't forget such a beautiful woman."

"No, we haven't met. I'm Sissy Covington." Sissy lifted her champagne flute with her left hand.

Emerson changed tactics after he stared at Sissy's engagement ring. "Well, it's wonderful to meet you. Do you and your fiancé work with an investment banker? It's never too early to combine your finances. I'd love to meet with both of you to discuss how I can help you with your future."

"How thoughtful of you to offer. Why don't you give me your card so that my fiancé can call you?" Sissy smiled so brightly that I almost felt sorry for Emerson. Rob would call Emerson, but it wouldn't be about his and Sissy's finances.

"Here you go. Looking forward to chatting with you." Emerson handed Sissy his card. "Excuse me, I need to go speak to Gideon about the gala for my aunt."

Emerson hurried toward Gideon on the other side of the courtyard. A woman in a blue cocktail dress who had been standing near us scooted over.

"Take this for what it's worth, but don't give Emerson your money," she said.

"Why?" Sissy widened her eyes. "Has he gotten into trouble?"

"Not that I know of, but I can tell you firsthand he's a terrible money manager." She frowned, then sipped her champagne. "And a worse date."

"Oh, honey, do tell." Sissy lowered her voice.

"Emerson has moved from company to company. I was his client at his last bank, and he made stupid mistakes. Fortunately, I didn't lose much money. But I lost time going on a few dates with him." The woman downed the rest of her champagne. "He's a gentleman, and if he gets his head on straight, he'd be a decent banker. But he can't change who his momma is."

"Oh, is she the overbearing type?" Sissy asked.

"She's the no-one-is-good-enough-for-my-baby type." The woman laughed. "One dinner with her and Emerson, and I knew it would never work out. If you marry Emerson, you marry his momma, too. No thanks."

"Thank goodness I wasn't interested in him as a financial advisor or date." Sissy laughed.

"I'd say you're set on both counts with that ring." The woman pointed at Sissy's engagement ring and then turned to me. "Now, I am worried about you. I don't see a ring on you, and I saw Emerson kiss you. Be careful around him."

"I will." And I meant it. I was quite happy with Connor and my financial advisor, but even if I wasn't, I wouldn't be interested in Emerson. Not only because of his personality, but he could also be a killer.

We almost made it out of the courtyard, but Gideon spotted us.

"Ladies, hello! I'm so happy y'all finally came to one of my art shows." Gideon rushed over to us. "What do you think of my home and the art?"

"Your home showcases the art." I managed not to tell him my true feelings about his home.

"Yes, what Sammy said." Sissy put her arm through mine.

"Are you friends with Emerson Merritt? We were so surprised to see him here, considering his cousin died yesterday," I said.

"You know him? You're engaged, Sissy, so you're not romantically interested in him." Gideon grinned. "How about you, Samantha? Are you interested in trading in your trumpet player for a man in finance?"

"Absolutely not," I laughed, not taking offense at Gideon's question.

"Glad to hear it." Gideon lowered his voice. "He's a decent man, but he just can't seem to keep a job or a woman for long. At least he's an excellent son and nephew."

"He told us he was here tonight because of his Aunt Lydia," Sissy said.

"Lydia Townsend could write a book on etiquette, but she tends to take it to the extreme. No one expects her to come to an event the day after her daughter passes." Gideon shook his head. "Perhaps it was just a distraction for her. But then again, she loves going to all the charity events."

"She must be passionate about helping others," Sissy said.

"What she does like is being in the spotlight at the meetings. Oh, I know that sounds terrible, but it's true. I don't believe she ever had a career except taking care of her husband and daughter. After he passed away, she joined a boatload of organizations. From our art group to cat rescues to saving the rainforest, Lydia joined every group that would have her."

"It sounds like she's quite the philanthropist," I said.

"Oh, she is in spirit, but she's tightened her pocketbook over the years. If you get my drift." Gideon glanced around the room. "Her trust fund is dwindling. Poor thing. She tried to get her daughter to help, but Paige said no."

"Gideon, we're running out of champagne!" Skye, Gideon's assistant, rushed over to him.

"Skye, simmer down. There's more in the butler's pantry." Gideon sighed heavily.

"No, Gideon, there isn't any more there. Don't you think I would check there first?" Skye ran her hand through her sparkling lilac-colored hair.

"Fine. Let's check the storage room." Gideon frowned. "And wipe your hands, Skye. You've got that ridiculous glitter on you. I hate glitter."

The two of them left us, arguing over glitter and where

the champagne could be. Sissy and I left the party, not arguing but going over all the information we learned tonight. It seemed as if both Emerson and Lydia needed money. But would either of them kill for it?

17

"Happy Birthday, my sweet niece!" Aunt Charlene entered Lagniappe Books at 9 a.m., with a large vase of stargazer lilies blocking her face. But I didn't need to see it to know she was smiling. Her voice bubbled with enthusiasm as she handed the flowers to Andrew.

"Thanks, Aunt Charlene," I sputtered as she tightly embraced me. She hugged me tighter than she usually did.

"Momma, let Sammy breathe." Jasper mouthed, "Sorry" to me over his shoulder.

"I'm just happy we can celebrate your birthday, Sammy! I mean, one of your birthdays." Aunt Charlene took the vase from Andrew who raised his eyebrows at me. We had just made a bet when Aunt Charlene would come to wish me a happy birthday. He won with his time of nine fifteen. I had said ten thirty, so now I owed him a box of pralines.

Today was my real birthday. I had always wondered what day it was, but it hadn't been as important as knowing who my birth family were and what had happened to me as a two-year-old. Now that I had those answers, knowing my actual birthday was just another part of my history. I didn't feel the need to celebrate it. My legal birthday was just fine to celebrate. And funnily enough , it turned out they were just a few days apart.

"It's very sweet of you to come here so early, and with flowers," I said.

"And beignets and café au lait." Jasper headed toward the back seating area with a tray of cups and a bag of beignets.

Andrew designed the shop to be similar to a home library. Mahogany shelves lined the walls filled with every genre possible. A large dining room table served as our sales counter. In the rear of the store was a seating area with the comfortable burgundy love seat, along with two matching chairs, and a low marble coffee table.

"Now, I brought the flowers here because they're poisonous to cats. We have to keep the Thibodeaux Mansion kitties safe." Aunt Charlene fiddled with the arrangement after she placed them on the coffee table.

"I told Momma not to make a big deal out of today, but you know her." Jasper sat down next to his mother on the couch. Andrew and I sat in the side chairs and accepted cups of coffee from Jasper.

"It's all right. I appreciate how much y'all care." I opened the bag of beignets, letting the sweet scent of powdered sugar on fried dough fill the air. Andrew brought china plates out from the office for the beignets as well as linen napkins. This wasn't just in honor of my birthday; he preferred to do everything with panache.

"See, I told you." Aunt Charlene jabbed Jasper on his shoulder. "But we didn't just come here for your birthday. I think you should go see Momo and Nora today."

"Did something happen after we left last night?" I

dropped my beignet, causing a poof of powdered sugar to scatter on the plate.

"No, no, nothing new, honey." Aunt Charlene reached over the coffee table patted my hand, leaving streaks of sugar. "They could just use a bit of your sweetness."

"And an update on your investigation, I bet," Jasper said.

"I'm not investigating..."

All three of them laughed. My first inclination was to protest again, but I gave up. "Fine, fine, you three. Yes, I've asked around a bit. But I'm not getting into trouble."

"You better not," Aunt Charlene and Andrew said in unison.

"If Momma and Andrew both agree, you better listen, Cousin." Jasper grinned.

"Let's just enjoy the beignets and coffee without any talk of mysteries," I said. "I promise I'll be on my best behavior."

I sank back into my chair and sipped my café au lait, enjoying the slight bitterness of the smooth chicory coffee. Between my real job and my role as an amateur detective, I would need all the coffee I could get today.

Before everyone left for Thanksgiving celebrations the next day, we decided to meet at The Gas Light. In our group text, I let everyone know that I was stopping by Momo's house first.

"Oh, good, you remembered to visit." Aunt Charlene opened the door and pulled me inside. She lowered her voice. "Lydia is visiting with Nora. By the sounds of it, Nora could use an interruption."

Before I could ask her what she meant, I heard the raised voices coming from down the hall. Momo paced outside Nora's door. Lady Clementine sat off to the side, watching Momo intently.

"I can't decide if I should go in and break it up," Momo whispered after Aunt Charlene and I tiptoed down the hall. "I can't hear every word, but they did say Hollis's and Paige's names."

"Sammy, go in there." Aunt Charlene put her hand on the small of my back and pushed me. I caught my balance before I ran into the the bedroom door.

"Aunt Charlene, I'm not interrupting them," I grumbled. "If anyone is going to, it should be Momo."

Before the three of us could argue about it, Lydia shouted, "You took Hollis away from me and now Paige. How could you, Nora?"

Lydia flung open the door and barreled into me. "Sorry, I, um, have to leave."

"How could you say that to Nora? There is no reason to be cruel to her," Momo reprimanded Lydia, her eyes full of fury.

Lydia covered her mouth with her hands and then rushed down the hall. She fumbled with the lock on the front door and then let out a sob.

"Now, Momo, remember, she just lost her daughter. When you're bogged down with grief, it's easy to forget your manners." Aunt Charlene put her arm around Momo's shoulders.

"You're right." Momo dropped her chin to her chest. "Will you check on her while I go see Nora?"

"I will. You two go see Nora," I said. Hearing Nora's soft sobs coming from her room, she needed company. And while I was concerned about Lydia's state of mind, I definitely wanted to know why she accused Nora of taking her brother and daughter away from her.

Momo and Aunt Charlene entered Nora's bedroom and I went to Lydia.

"Let me help you with the door, Mrs. Townsend," I said.

Lydia robotically stepped back from the door without saying a word.

"Here you go." I opened the door and stood back to make room for Lydia to leave. She didn't move but looked down the hall. The bedroom door was shut, and no sounds were audible from our spot.

"I was so cruel to Nora." Lydia took a tissue from her purse. "I should go apologize, but I doubt she would accept it."

"Give her time," I said gently. "In our moments of grief, we say all kinds of things we don't mean."

"Yes, yes, of course, but I had no right to blame her for Paige's death. What happened to Paige might have happened even if she had her medical bag with her." Lydia stuffed the tissue in her purse.

"What do you mean if she had her medical bag?" I said.

"We wondered, if Paige had her medical bag, would her killer have just taken the drugs and left her alive?" she said.

"Do the police believe she was murdered because she didn't have any drugs with her?" This was news to me.

"Well, no. They might, but Emerson and Dorothy believe it." Lydia stared at the floor.

"So they believe someone tried to rob Paige and since she didn't have the bag, they killed her?" It was a valid theory.

"Dorothy says it was Paige's boyfriend, but I just don't believe it. Even though I didn't think he was the best choice for her, he treated her with respect." Lydia raised her head and opened her mouth but didn't speak. She quickly snapped her mouth closed and fidgeted with her purse.

"Can you think of anyone else who would want to hurt your daughter?" I asked gently, hoping that a calm voice would help her speak the truth.

Lydia shook her head, making her diamond-drop earrings clink softly. "It must have been a stranger. Now, if you'll excuse me, I need to get home."

"Would you like me to walk you home or call a cab for you?" I asked.

"No, thank you, but I appreciate your kindness." Lydia's face softened. "Could you please apologize to Nora for me?"

"Of course." I said to the back of Lydia's head as she climbed down the stairs quickly.

She hurried down the street, keeping a steady pace as she weaved in and out of the pedestrians on the sidewalk. As I closed the door, I thought about what Lydia said. Did she really believe it was a stranger like her sister and nephew? She didn't appear to believe Paige's boyfriend had anything to do with it. But how did she feel about Emerson and Dorothy? Did she believe one of them murdered her daughter? Or was she throwing suspicion toward anyone else to protect herself?

18

"I'm so excited to go to your favorite bar!" Aunt Charlene trilled as we walked to The Gas Light.

Momo and Aunt Charlene had already left Nora's room when I closed the front door. Nora asked for privacy, so they did as she wished. The exhaustion showed in Momo's face, but she insisted she was fine. She planned to relax with a glass of bourbon in the living room.

"Go out with Sammy, Charlene. I'll call you if I need help." Momo's firm voice and rigid face stopped Aunt Charlene in mid-protest.

When Aunt Charlene left to get her purse, Momo said, "I hope you don't mind me sending Charlene with you. Don't get me wrong, she's a big help, but I could use some time to myself."

"That I understand." I grinned. "Call me if you need anything at all."

I left quietly as Momo sunk into the living room couch and rested her eyes.

"This is it? It's as plain as my memaw's grits." Aunt Charlene frowned as she stood in front of the bar. I had the same first impression except for the comparison to grits. The exterior was nondescript with only a gaslight and a hand-painted sign that said "The Gas Light. 21 and over only."

I opened the door, and Aunt Charlene's frown disappeared. "Now, this looks like a bar! How darling!"

I doubted anyone had entered The Gas Light and called it darling. Not that the bar was a dark, downtrodden place, but it wasn't fancy by any means. A mix of round and square tables filled the narrow but deep room. A well-worn wooden bar ran the length of the room. Every stool at the bar was adorned with backpacks, tool belts, and purses. Flickering along the right side of the room were the bar's namesake gaslights. The Gas Light's interior was bright and warm but far from cutesy.

Aunt Charlene walked through like she owned the place. She smiled as she squeezed through the tables, but stopped at my friend Terry Faucheaux's table. He and his friend Jimmy held court at this table regularly to play poker. They used a bowl of stale peanuts as their chips, so they never exchanged any money. I held my breath as Terry did his trademark greeting to a bar newcomer.

"Excuse me, miss. Have you seen any teeth lying around?" Terry gave her his wide, toothless smile. "If you see them soaking in a beer mug, will you give it to me?"

The chatter in the room grew quiet as everyone waited for Aunt Charlene's response. Most newcomers came with a regular patron, so they were pre-warned about Terry's gimmick. I should have said something to Aunt Charlene, but by the sparkle in her eyes, it wasn't necessary.

"Oh, darling, I hope you find them. You'd be so handsome with your teeth." Aunt Charlene patted Terry's shoulder. "You think about that and maybe then I'll play poker with you."

She winked and sashayed toward the back, where our friends were waiting. A smattering of laughter filled the room, but everyone returned to their previous conversations. Terry's eyes followed Aunt Charlene. Jimmy reached over and pushed Terry's mouth back up.

"You better close your mouth, or whatever brain cells you have left are going to fly out." Jimmy laughed. "Come on, Terry, she's not the first woman to stand up to your stupid 'I'm a toothless guy just drinking beers and playing cards' shtick."

"You're right, but isn't she prettier than a mess of fried catfish?" Terry said.

"Is that a compliment?" I asked. There were so many Southern phrases I hadn't heard.

"Oh, yes, it is. I'd say our Terry is smitten."

"You're right." Terry popped his teeth back in his mouth, wiped his hands on a cocktail napkin, and stood up. "Sammy, what does your aunt like to drink?"

"Um, a piña colada, but are you really going to ask Rose to make it?"

The Gas Light wasn't known for the cocktails Rose called "froo froo." A large variety of beers, simple cocktails like a whiskey sour on the rocks, and two types of wine— one red, one white—made up the bar's offerings. There was a blender, and when someone dared to order a drink that required it, the entire bar stopped chatting at the rare sound.

"I sure am. Or I'll make it myself." Terry kissed me on the cheek before heading to the bar.

"Well, well. I've only seen Terry act like this three times before." Jimmy grinned. "Your Aunt Charlene could be Terry's next wife."

Terry wasn't the only one interested in someone.

"Now, Sammy, tell me all about your friend Terry." Aunt Charlene patted the seat next to her. "Jasper says you're friends with him and that he actually has teeth."

Jasper's face was a mixture of amusement and horror. His father passed a few years ago, and Charlene and her friend Gigi had met many eligible bachelors on their Caribbean cruises. While Gigi snagged a live-in boyfriend, Charlene enjoyed flirting only. "I'm a fantastic catch, but I need some time to myself. I went from my momma and daddy's house to one with my husband. Now I can be on my own and do whatever I want. Can you believe I actually eat ice cream in bed?" The look of satisfaction on her face made me smile. As overbearing as she could be, I loved Aunt Charlene. Enough so that I could overlook her occasional inappropriate comment or critique.

I gave Aunt Charlene as much information about Terry as I could. To be fair, it wasn't a lot. I knew Terry grew up outside New Orleans on a bayou. He loved telling stories of fighting and fishing with his cousin Bobby. He talked about his grandaddy's still. Terry was one of those people who you felt like you had known forever when you met him. He was funny, kind, and never at a loss for words.

From his friend Jimmy, I discovered he owned The Gas Light. Since I was sworn to secrecy, I didn't tell my aunt.

Terry was well known for his artistic career, especially since he had his paintings displayed at Libby's café until the end of the year. And I was certain he'd been married at least three times and was now single.

"My, he sounds like an interesting man." Aunt Charlene turned in her chair to face Terry's table. He and Jimmy were deep into a poker game, with Terry's pile of stale peanuts growing higher.

"Yes, he is." Rose Hebert came up to our table with one drink in her hand. "And he is quite the gentleman. Here is a piña colada just for you, Charlene."

"Oh, my goodness! I just love piña coladas!" Aunt Charlene took the cocktail and took a sip. "My goodness, Rose, this is the best one I've ever had. You're such a doll. Thank you!"

Rose's eyes shone, rivaling the sparkle of her rings. Her chunky jewelry contrasted with the pastel-colored clothes she wore every day. Rose was tough as nails when it came to running the bar, but she had a big heart and a soft spot for her boyfriend, Neal.

"Don't thank me. Terry sent over the drink for you. He hopes you'll accept his apology for his prank." Rose raised her eyebrows. "Terry has teeth, in case you were wondering."

"Well then, I should go over and thank him for the delicious drink." Aunt Charlene pushed back her chair and flipped her hair over her shoulder. "Y'all don't mind, do you?"

"Of course not," I answered.

"Should I be your chaperone, Aunt Charlene?" Neal put his beer on the table. "We wouldn't want your reputation to be besmirched."

"Besmirched? Oh, Neal, you're a hoot." My aunt kissed

Neal on top of his head. "I think I can handle myself. Unless Jasper thinks I need help."

"No, I'm not worried about you, Momma. Just be nice to Terry, though. We like this bar a lot." Jasper took a big swig of his beer.

Aunt Charlene giggled and picked up her drink. We all turned and watched her approach the table. Terry sprang up and pulled out a chair for her. They began chatting right away. Jimmy looked over at us and gave us a thumbs-up.

"Does your mom play poker, Jasper?" Rose asked.

"Yep. She's a great player, but she acts like she doesn't understand the game at first." Jasper smiled. "Terry and Jimmy won't know what hit them."

"This will be fun to watch," Rose said. "But first, what would you like to drink, Sammy? Is it a Pimm's Cup night, or do you want a piña colada, too?"

I wrinkled my nose. "Piña coladas are way too sweet. I'll come with you and decide there."

Rose returned to the bar, and I settled on an empty stool.

"All right, you are having a Pimm's Cup. I can tell you want one. So to what do I owe the pleasure of your presence at the bar?" Rose started making my drink as she spoke.

"No one gets anything past you, do they?" I drummed my fingers on the bar. "Neal told me you threw Tate King out of here one time."

"I was wondering when you were going to ask me about him." Rose put my drink on the bar. "Neal said you wanted some information on him. I read about Paige Townsend's death, so I assume Tate is a suspect."

"I think so." Rob and Christine hadn't confirmed any suspects. But if they were trying to track him down, he must be one of them.

"Take this for what it's worth, but I doubt he killed her.

In his drunken stupor, he said he loved her and wished he hadn't messed up," Rose said. "Never say never, but the last time I saw him, Paige was with him."

"When was that?"

"About three months ago. They came into the bar and Tate apologized for his behavior. He looked healthy and sober."

"And Paige was with him?" I asked.

"Yes. I heard she went with him to two other bars. He apologized to them, too," Rose said.

"I wonder if he did it because Paige made him?"

"She might have, but she stayed by the door. But I heard from the bartenders at Randall's that he's hanging out there again."

"I wonder if Paige knew about that," I said.

"She did, because she was with him there last week. I was there with my sister and saw them." Rose leaned closer to me over the bar. "Listen, not all recovering alcoholics avoid bars. You'd be surprised how many people come here to socialize with their friends. I make sure we always have nonalcoholic beer."

"You're a thoughtful bartender, Rose. And person."

"It's the right thing to do." Rose smiled. "Paige and Tate can go to the bar without drinking undetected. Or care."

"Rose, I'm dying here!" Bob, a regular, shouted from the other end of the bar.

"Oh, please. You're such a liar." Rose rolled her eyes. "Duty calls. I'll talk to you later, Sammy."

From Rose's information, it didn't sound like Paige and Tate were having issues, at least none in public. I needed to talk to Tate, and I bet I would find him at Randall's.

But I couldn't tonight. This was our own "Friendsgiving" minus the holiday food. Connor and his parents were going to visit relatives as was Sissy. Andrew and Beau were holding down the fort at Hotel Jeanne so as many of the employees could spend time at home. Rose offered to work on Thanksgiving so she would be here with Neal keeping her company. Next year we all promised to host a huge Thanksgiving dinner at Thibodeaux Mansion.

As I joined my friends over at our table, I reminded myself that I was fortunate to spend this time with my family and friends before we all went our own ways for Thanksgiving. Paige couldn't share the holiday with her friends and family, but I could.

19

———

"**Y**ou must be joking! No one would think to make sweet potatoes that way!" Momo put her glass of bourbon on the dining table with a thud and covered her mouth as she laughed.

"No, I'm not! My great-great Uncle Elias decided he would finally bring a dish to Thanksgiving. Given he was a confirmed bachelor, nobody expected him to bring a dish. His moonshine was all anyone wanted." Aunt Charlene wiped her hands on her apron. "And after making his version of sweet potatoes, moonshine was all he was allowed to bring."

"It's true. I was there." Jasper shuddered. "There is nothing worse than lumpy mashed potatoes mixed with orange juice. There was nothing sweet about them."

Everyone in Momo's dining room roared with laughter. Jasper, Aunt Charlene, and I had planned to celebrate the holiday together in my apartment. Aunt Charlene proposed we spend the day with Momo and Nora. We decided it would be easier to eat at Momo's house, since my apartment was small. And it would make it easier for Nora, too.

Lydia and Dorothy also invited Nora and Momo to join them, but they declined. "They did it because it was the right thing to do according to the Southern way. But they were relieved when we said no," Momo had said.

So it was the five of us here in Momo's elegant dining room. Momo set the table with her mother's daisy-motif china, actual sterling silverware, and crystal glasses. She sat at the head of the table, although she offered it to Jasper, who refused. "If I sit there, you're going to make me carve the turkey. If you'd seen the way I carve pumpkins, you won't ask me to do the turkey."

"I figured I would do it, but Momo, this is your home, so you sit at the head of the table." Aunt Charlene patted Momo on the shoulder. "I'll carve it in the kitchen and bring out a platter. Jasper and Sammy will help carry everything to the table."

Jasper and I brought out the side dishes as Aunt Charlene worked on the turkey. My green bean casserole made with canned soup didn't have a chance next to Aunt Charlene's oyster dressing created from scratch. Jasper made the mashed potatoes, but not "sweet potatoes" like his great-great-great Uncle Elias.

He and I fought over which kind of cranberry relish to have, so we had both canned and Frankie's homemade relish. I had stopped at Frankie's shop earlier in the week to buy her relish and dinner rolls.

"This all smells so good, Charlene," Nora inhaled deeply as Jasper placed the last dish on the table.

"I can't take all the credit. Sammy and Jasper helped." Charlene took her seat to the left of Momo.

"I helped with the mashed potatoes," Jasper said.

"Yes, darling, you peeled them so well. You only nicked your fingers twice this year." Charlene smiled at her son.

"Do I need to check the mashed potatoes before we eat them?" I grinned at Jasper.

"Only if I should check your sweet potato pie for eggshells. Things were flying all over your kitchen this morning." Jasper laughed. "Just kidding!"

I set down the roll I feigned throwing at him. I wouldn't waste one on him. Also, I doubted Momo would appreciate if we started a food fight.

"Okay, you two," Momo laughed. "Nora, do you remember when Hollis brought over Emerson for dinner one night?"

"How could I forget?" Nora's face lit up. "Hollis was so nervous that he dropped the basket of rolls on the way to the table."

"And then during dinner, Emerson grabbed a roll we'd missed and threw it across the table at Hollis. It knocked over that candlestick and chipped it." Momo pointed to one of the blue-and-yellow-floral-patterned ceramic candlestick holders on the table.

I sat closest to the candlestick and reached over and noted a chip in the base. Not a large one, but it marred the candlestick's perfect shape.

"Hollis turned beet red. I had to press my hand on his shoulder to keep him still." Nora looked up at the ceiling. "He was already mad that he had to take Emerson's cars away from him and now he'd caused damage."

"Took away his cars?" Jasper asked.

"Emerson used to carry these little metal race cars everywhere he went. He would scatter them all over the courtyard when he played out there," Nora said.

"Hollis made Emerson apologize, which he did grudgingly. His mother came by the next day to offer her own, which she also did grudgingly," Momo said.

"I didn't know that," Nora said.

"It wasn't worth mentioning. Emerson was a feisty child and didn't like to follow the rules. Dorothy believed he was incapable of doing anything wrong, so she tried to cover for him as best she could."

"What's the saying here? Tru dat?" Nora said.

We all laughed and continued on with our delicious meal. As I ate another bite of oyster dressing, I wondered if Dorothy was still covering for her son.

"As Hollis used to say, I'm as fat as a tick. This was an amazing meal." Nora patted her mouth with her napkin. "I need a nap before dessert, unless anyone objects."

"May I help you to your room, Miss Nora?" Jasper jumped up and stood by Nora before I could even move.

"Such a gentleman, thank you, Jasper." Nora accepted Jasper's hand and let him lead her out of the dining room.

"Thank you for making this such a wonderful holiday." Momo's eyes teared up when Jasper returned to the table. "Spending the day laughing and enjoying friendship is such a pleasure for Nora and for me."

"And for us, too, darling." Aunt Charlene smiled brightly at Momo. "Perhaps this would be a good time to tell Jasper and Sammy about our plans."

Jasper and I looked at each other in confusion.

"You two make the same look when you don't know what's going on." Momo laughed. "I'm not running off to join Charlene on her cruises. At least not yet."

I bit my tongue not to laugh out loud at the image of Momo dressed like my aunt on her cruises. Momo didn't strike me as the bright-colored-sundress-with-matching-sun-hat woman who drank piña coladas and played shuffleboard.

"I'm staying with Momo to help with Nora," Aunt Charlene said.

"She's been a godsend, and I really don't want to spend the time finding someone else to help," Momo said.

"How long did the doctors give Nora?" Jasper said.

Momo's shoulders sagged. "Anywhere from days to weeks to months. Paige thought Nora had at least another month."

"Now, I'm no doctor or nurse, but I'd agree with Paige. Nora has something that's keeping her on this earth," Aunt Charlene said.

Momo locked eyes with me, and I had to force myself from shrinking in my chair. No pressure at all, Momo.

Aunt Charlene continued speaking: "My memaw was just the same. She wanted to see the sun rise over the cotton fields one more time. I took her out there. Seeing the peace spread over her face as the sun grew brighter...well, it was just something special."

My aunt took a tissue from her dress pocket and dabbed at her eyes. "But what was even more special was when she told me she and pawpaw had their first kiss out there and their last argument out there. She just needed to apologize to him for that fight because he died that afternoon. Of course, it wasn't because of that argument. Pawpaw drank enough whiskey to pickle his liver three times over. But it wasn't until she remembered how beautiful the cotton field had been most of her life that she felt peace. She passed away the next day at sunrise. God's truth."

A stillness filled the room after Aunt Charlene finished her story. Jasper went to his mother and hugged her shoulders. "You've got a big heart, Momma."

"I agree." Momo raised her glass. "Here's to Charlene! Thank you for coming to help this old lady in her time of need."

We all raised our glasses to Charlene, the newest member of the French Quarter. At least until Momo no longer needed help with Nora. Jasper and I had talked before about the chance of his mother moving to New Orleans. This would be a good test to see how it would go. We'll be fine unless Aunt Charlene tries to control me and Jasper. Shouldn't we?

20

"You're yawning already? It's only eight." Andrew handed me a cup of coffee. "We have a long day ahead."

"I've been up for three hours already, thank you very much." I blew off the steam swirling up from the cup. "I tried to get back to sleep, but Nubi decided if I was up, he needed breakfast, and then it was playtime with his newest catnip toy."

"What was on your mind so early this morning?" Andrew sat down on the love seat. The shop wasn't opening until nine thirty, so we had a little time to chat.

I filled him in on Thanksgiving dinner at Momo's house, ending with the news that Aunt Charlene would stay to help with Nora.

"Is that's what bothering you? Considering your aunt can be overbearing at times, I understand your trepidation about her living here, even temporarily," Andrew said sympathetically.

"Yes, I'll admit to be a bit nervous, but she promised she

would be too busy caring for Nora and Momo and playing poker with Terry and Jimmy."

"Playing poker with Terry and Jimmy? What did I miss the other night?" Andrew's eyes widened.

"Sorry, I forgot to tell you." I laughed. "Terry tried his toothless-old-man routine on Aunt Charlene, but she didn't fall for it. But he fell for her."

"That is quite the news. Beau and I will keep her company, too, if she'll let us. I'm afraid we don't play poker, though." Andrew grinned.

"Maybe we should all learn so we can make sure Aunt Charlene stays out of trouble."

"Oh, she appears to handle herself just fine. And it's temporary, right?"

I nodded, hoping it was temporary. I'm not sure how Jasper and I would handle Aunt Charlene being in town for an extended time. But hopefully she will be, because that would mean Nora still needed her. The longer Nora was alive, the longer I had to figure out if Nora killed Hollis.

A firm knock startled Andrew and me as we finished closing up the shop. "I'll see who it is. "Andrew pulled back the curtain on the front door. He didn't hesitate and unlocked the door. I assumed it was Miss Ruth, a frequent patron, who always arrived as we were closing. Instead, it was Dorothy.

"Mrs. Merritt, please come in."

Dorothy, dressed in a black wool pantsuit, held a vase of yellow roses. "Thank you, Mr. Ballard. I'm sorry to intrude, but Momo told me I would find Samantha here."

"It's not an intrusion. Please accept my sincere condolences on your loss." Andrew gestured for Dorothy to enter the shop. He closed the door behind her.

"Thank you." She walked toward me. "I wanted to thank you Samantha, for your help. If Lydia had found Paige alone, she would have collapsed." I accepted the flowers from her and noticed a slight tremor in her hands.

"I'm glad I could help. How is Mrs. Townsend?"

"As good as expected. She's quite embarrassed about her behavior at Momo's two nights ago." Dorothy pressed her hands against her stomach. "I'm thankful Nora and Momo understand it was her grief talking. You do, too, I hope."

"I do. I can only imagine the pain of losing your child," I said.

"It must be devastating." Andrew took the vase from me and placed it on the sales table. "Would you like to sit down? I am happy to make you and Samantha a cup of tea."

"No, thank you. I should return to Lydia. But first I wanted to ask if you had heard anything about the investigation from the police, Samantha."

"N-no," I stammered. Why in the world was she asking me about Paige's case?

"Oh." She pursed her lips. "Since you're close to Detectives Gammon and Armstrong, I assumed you'd have more information than the family."

"I'm sorry, but we haven't spoken," I said.

"Detectives Armstrong and Gammon are excellent detectives, I can assure you." Andrew stepped next to me. "I'm sure they would answer any questions you and your family have about their investigation."

"Of course. I merely hoped you might have heard something. They must feel that they need to spare us of any dreadful details." Dorothy took a tissue from her matching purse and dabbed at her eyes. "I just wondered if they spoke with Paige's ex-boyfriend, Tate King."

"Do you suspect he had something to do with Paige's death?" I asked.

"Possibly." Dorothy inhaled deeply. "He and Paige met in a rehabilitation clinic, so he may have gone to her for drugs. And since she didn't have her medical bag, perhaps he became angry and killed her."

"I assume you've told this to the detectives, Mrs. Merritt," Andrew said.

"Oh, yes, I did. I just hope they took the information seriously. Not that I want Momo to feel bad if this happened to Paige," Dorothy said.

Andrew put his arm around me, either to comfort me or to keep me from yelling in Dorothy's face. How dare she act like Momo had anything to do with Paige's death.

"I'm sure the detectives are looking at all possibilities, Mrs. Merritt." Andrew's tone was noticeably sharp.

"Yes, of course." Dorothy tucked her tissue into her purse. "Thank you again for your help, Samantha. Happy Thanksgiving to you both."

"And to you and Mrs. Townsend." Andrew walked with her and opened the door for her. She left without another word.

"How can she blame Momo for Paige's death?" I huffed after Andrew locked the door. "That's totally not fair. No one has ever mentioned Tate trying to get anything from Paige."

"Calm down, Samantha. Even if she meant it, it doesn't matter. Momo is not responsible for Paige's death." Andrew hugged me. "Although I don't have your detective sensibility, I can confidently say I think Dorothy is trying to throw responsibility off her family and on to anyone else. It's not right, but let's give her the benefit of the doubt and say she's just under an unfathomable amount of stress."

"You're right. We should give her the benefit of the doubt," I lied, not wanting to argue with Andrew. I was too tired, but Dorothy's actions and words made me question her honesty. Was she involved in Paige's murder? Or could she be the actual killer?

I needed more information from another source. Tonight, I needed to go find Tate King.

21

I was still fuming when I arrived at Thibodeaux Mansion. But the sight of Sissy feeding the cats changed my mood.

"You are spoiling them." I sat down at my bistro table across from Sissy. "Does Ruby know how many treats you give them?"

"No. Unless Cleopatra and Nefertiti have told her." Sissy put more snacks in front of the three cats. "Or you or Nubi."

"I'm shocked you'd even consider Nubi or me capable of something like that." Nubi meowed, apparently in agreement.

"I'm sorry, Nubi. And you, too, Sammy." Sissy's face broke into a huge grin.

"I swear Nubi is your best friend, not me." I picked up Nubi and held him like a baby.

"You're too funny. Do I go on escapades with Nubi?" Sissy reached over the table and scratched Nubi's little white patch of fur.

"Not that I know of." I laughed. "Speaking of escapades, I have one to go on tonight."

"Give me the details," Sissy said.

"I need to talk to Paige's boyfriend, Tate. Her family is throwing him under the bus for the murder," I said.

"And you don't think he did it?"

"I'm not sure." I placed Nubi on the ground and leaned back in my chair. "Dorothy and Emerson always bring him up, which I guess is natural. But something about them makes me think they're grasping at straws. I can't explain it."

"That's your intuition and you should always listen to it." Sissy stood up. "Let's talk to Tate and get his side of the story."

"Really? You're the best." I hugged her.

"After a day of shopping with my momma, I could use a drink."

"Well, it might not be much of a break."

"Honey, you don't know what shopping is like with Momma. Going to talk with one of your suspects is a break." Sissy laughed.

"Remember, it's your fiancé's suspect, too. I don't want to put you in a difficult position."

"Don't you worry. We just are going to a new place for drinks. What's the bar?"

"Randall's in the Bywater."

"Oh, they have a huge beer selection. That's our excuse if we need one," Sissy said.

"Well then, let's go."

"There it is." Sissy pointed to a one-story corner building on the corner of Dauphine Street and Gallier Street. Weathered wood siding in white covered both sides of the bar. Like The Gas Light, it sported a simple sign by the entrance. The interior was also like our bar, with its eclectic selection of wood tables and chairs. To the right of the entrance was the wood bar lined with stools. Two long shelves held beer bottles, while another shelf held liquor bottles. A chalkboard to the left of the shelves listed six beers on draft.

I recognized Tate King from the vintage blue-and-white varsity jacket he wore the night I saw him with Paige. He sat on the last stool at the far end of the bar. Sissy and I claimed the two empty stools beside him.

"Cop or reporter?" Tate snapped as I sat down.

"Excuse me?" I said.

"Cop or reporter?" He took a long sip of his beer. "I've never seen you here before, and you came right to me. What do you want?"

I considered lying and saying he was mistaken. But a casual conversation with him, aimed at getting him to talk naturally about Paige, seemed fruitless at this point. Time to jump right in and be honest.

"I'm neither, but I do have questions for you. My name is Samantha Richardson. I was with Lydia Townsend when she found Paige. I was there to return her medical bag for Momo McBride. Paige worked for her."

"You were there? The police said someone was with Lydia, but not who." Tate gulped the last half of the beer in his glass. "Did she look like she suffered?"

"No, I imagine she died quickly." I didn't know that, but from the pain in Tate's eyes, that's the answer he needed. Of course, he might already know that if he killed her.

"That's a small relief, I guess." Tate stared vacantly at the wall behind the bar. "I'm aware of who Momo is. Paige talked about her and her patient, Nora, all the time. She liked them."

"They both loved her. I only met Paige once, but I could

see how much she cared about them." I turned toward the bartender, who had come over to me. "Hey, Tammy, I didn't realize you worked here."

"This is my second job. Being an artist doesn't always pay the bills." Tammy sighed. "But next year I'm doing a show at Libby's, so that might get me out of this gig."

Libby supported local artists by hosting art shows at her café. She was an artist herself but preferred to showcase others. Her heart matched the size of her cinnamon buns.

"That's fantastic. Exhibiting your work there will definitely help your career," Sissy said.

"Thanks." Tammy tucked a piece of her long pink hair behind her multi-pierced ear. "What can I get you two?"

"I'll have what Tate's having. Would you like another one?" I said.

"You don't want what I'm having," Tate scoffed.

I caught myself before I asked him why. Rose had said bars keep nonalcoholic beer, so I assumed he must be drinking one.

"Tammy, I'd love to try one of your beers on tap. Pick your favorite," Sissy said.

"Same for me, thanks," I said. "And add Tate's next drink on my tab."

"You don't have to do that to get me to talk." Tate turned to face me. "If you're friends with Momo, I'm going to assume you're trying to get info on me to see if I killed Paige."

I decided to be as blunt as Tate. "Yes, you're right. But also to learn more about Paige. Something doesn't sit right about her death."

"Now, that I agree on," he said.

"Listen, Tate. I'm a nurse, and I know that you and Paige met as fellow clients at..." Sissy said.

"You can say it. We met as patients at rehab. Neither of us kept it a secret," Tate said. "Her family wanted her to say she worked there."

"Let me guess: Paige's family didn't like you because of where you met," Sissy said.

"Bingo," Tate said.

"Paige's family alluded to issues in your relationship," I said.

"The few times we argued at Paige's place, her family would come out to check on her. They'd say they were worried I was drunk or on drugs." He shook his head. "I'm sober. And before you ask, I never abused her. I loved her. I never hurt her, and I didn't kill her."

He seemed sincere. His body language appeared appropriate for a grieving boyfriend. But I didn't know him. "Do you know of anyone who would want to hurt her?"

"I'll tell you what I told the cops. Look into that weird family of Paige's. They're obsessed with their status and reputation like we're still back in the 1800s." Tate grimaced.

"I've heard that about them," I said.

"Paige's cousin tows the family line with his expensive sports car and fancy office job. Paige drove a used car, wore ordinary clothes, and had a subservient job, in their eyes. And she wasn't married."

"Emerson isn't married," Sissy said.

"Yeah, but he's a man. He can sow his oats until the proper lady appears." He rolled his eyes. "So far, no one has met with Mommy's approval.

I felt even more sorry for Paige. It couldn't have been easy being the odd one out in her family.

"What else can you tell us about the them?" Sissy asked.

"Between keeping their perfect reputation intact and

struggling with finances, they have a lot more imperfections that they struggle to hide."

"What things are they hiding?" I said.

"Nothing that I want to talk about now." He checked his watch. "Sorry."

While I was disappointed, I decided not to push him on this. Hopefully if this conversation went well, he'd talk to me again. But I wasn't done asking questions tonight.

"Do you really believe someone in the family would kill her? For what reason?" I asked.

"I wouldn't put it past them. Paige told me about that weird thing her patient said about killing her uncle. Hollis Davenport is the end-all and be-all in that family, even as a dead man."

"Paige told me Nora just blurted it out, and it was a misunderstanding." I tapped my fingers on the bar. "You didn't believe Paige, did you?"

Tate's stare made the hairs on the back of my neck stand up. It wasn't his words, but it was the way he seemed to understand my thoughts that got to me.

"No. Paige was concerned about what Nora said. I walked her home from Momo's house, but she left me outside the courtyard gate. She told me she had to look for something in the storage room at her house," Tate said.

"She didn't tell you what it was?" I tried to keep the disappointment out of my voice. Knowing what she was searching for was important, especially since I saw the torn piece of paper in her hands that morning.

"It had to be about her uncle. She was so distracted on the way home. I don't think she even heard me when I said 'I love you' when she was closing the gate." Tate squeezed his eyes shut and gripped the edge of the bar.

Tammy brought over our drinks. She placed her hand

on Tate's. "It's all right. You're going to feel this way for a while, but your friends will get you through it."

"Thanks, Tammy." Tate opened his eyes and then looked at his watch. "If y'all don't mind, I need some time alone."

"Of course. Let me give you my number in case you think of anything else." I wrote my cell phone number on the back of my business card. "Again, I'm sorry about Paige."

"Me, too." Sissy slid off her stool and reached into her purse. Before I could stop her, she left money for our drinks and a large tip for Tammy.

Tate nodded and went back to his beer. We said goodbye to Tammy and headed for the door. Just as I reached for the handle, the door flew open. I barely had enough time to step back before being trampled.

"Sorry about that. Oh, it's you." Winston Briggs took off his trademark gray fedora hat and shook out his sandy-brown hair. "Why are you here? Has The Gas Light gotten too boring for you?"

"We're allowed to go to other bars," Sissy snapped.

"Yes, you are, as am I," Winston barked back at her. There was no love lost between these two. While Rob and Christine didn't need a defender, Sissy took it upon herself to critique Winston's negative posts about them and the police.

"Let's go, Sissy." I pulled her away from Winston and toward the door.

"I'm busy now, but I would like to talk to you, Sammy. I understand you were there when Paige's body was found." Winston smiled, which made him attractive, if you didn't know what a slimy journalist he was.

I pretended not to hear him and left with Sissy. Right before the door closed, I turned to see Winston taking a seat next to Tate. My heart sank as they shook hands. Winston took a journal and pen from his messenger bag and put his phone on the bar top.

Maybe I shouldn't have been so surprised Tate was talking to the media. He must want the killer found. Or was he trying to cover up his own tracks? I hoped my intuition held true, and he wasn't a killer. But right now, I wasn't so sure.

22

"Good morning, Sammy. And happy birthday as well." Mr. Hugo greeted me at the gates of St. Louis Cemetery No. 1. He handed me one of the paper coffee cups he held in his hands.

Today was my legal birthday. For some reason, I felt compelled to come to the cemetery. Maybe it was because I couldn't visit my adopted parents graves in Florda today. Or perhaps I needed to be with any parents and my birth ones were buried here. Whatever the case, here I was.

"Thanks. I'm surprised to see you here. I didn't realize you were back from your vacation."

Mr. Hugo was a security guard for the cemetery, but in the last few months he had reduced his schedule to two shifts a week. I sometimes called Mr. Hugo to open the cemetery early, so I came hoping whoever was on duty would be as nice.

"We got back yesterday. My wife has had enough of me, so she sent me back to work." Mr. Hugo's belly jiggled as he laughed. He reminded me of Santa Claus with his twinkling eyes and joyful disposition.

"I highly doubt that. It's more likely that you missed seeing Marie Laveau." I grinned.

"Oh, I made sure the other guards took care of her," Mr. Hugo said.

One of the most famous tombs in all of New Orleans was Marie Laveau's, the Voodoo queen. Visitors to the cemetery used to draw the letter X on the tomb in the hope that Marie Laveau would grant their wish. Mr. Hugo took extra care of her tomb as these Xs and a pink-paint vandal had damaged the mausoleum.

Mr. Hugo didn't practice Voodoo, but he had a healthy respect for those who did. He also dedicated himself to preserving the city's history and architecture.

"I'm sure they did." I laughed. "But thank you for being here early. Your shift doesn't start until eight a.m., doesn't it?"

"I'm only thirty minutes early. But don't thank me, thank your boyfriend. Connor texted me late last night to ask if I could go to the cemetery early. He felt you might appreciate some company."

Connor couldn't join me because he was returning from a trip. I would have been fine on my own, but I always appreciated Mr. Hugo's company.

"No matter how you ended up here, I'm glad to see you. Did you have a good time with your wife in San Francisco?" I said.

"We sure did, thanks to your recommendations. The missus loved everything. We rode the cable car every day. I'm glad you told us to walk on the Golden Gate Bridge. It sure was impressive."

Mr. Hugo had reduced his hours, so he and his wife could travel now and then. Before they went to San Francisco, he asked me for travel tips since I used to live there.

New Orleans was my favorite city, but I loved San Francisco. I loved the food and the landscape: New Orleans had better food, scenery, and, more importantly, a close and welcoming community. At least that was my experience. But I missed my friend Madeline in San Francisco. She promised to visit as soon as her daughter was older.

"I'm happy you had fun." I accepted Mr. Hugo's arm after he locked the gate behind us. We walked through the cemetery, careful not to twist our ankles on the uneven ground. Fractured concrete dotted the grass pathways. Now that I had been here multiple times, the ferns pushing their way out of the cracks in tombs didn't startle me. During my earlier visits to the cemetery, Mr. Hugo recounted the families laid to rest in the tombs and the cemetery's past. My knowledge of New Orleans cemeteries came from Mr. Hugo.

Visitors to St. Louis No. 1 would have tour guides sharing the history of those buried here. Homer Plessey and Marie Laveau are among the many famous Louisianans buried at St. Louis Cemetery No. 1. But not every mausoleum held famous people. The St. Martin tomb housed the last of my birth family.

We reached the tomb and began our ritual. Mr. Hugo always sang "Amazing Grace." He claimed it was for both me and the spirits. I can't say if any spirits liked it, but I did.

I visited the tomb often, but I struggled when I got here. The tomb listed my biological relatives, but I didn't remember any of them. Except my brother, whose name was the last on the list. Remembering him only brought me sorrow.

My name, which was engraved just before his, caused me even more pain. This name, Sarah Jane St. Martin, the one I learned of when I moved to New Orleans, was my birth name. Now and then, Aunt Charlene would slip and call me by that name. I stopped minding it when she did. For her and my cousin, Jasper, that's how they had thought of me. They hadn't known I had survived Hurricane Geoffrey and had a whole new life with my adopted parents.

Visiting the family tomb was the only physical connection I had to the family I had lost. I would come here and sit on the step, sometimes to talk, sometimes just to think. I was still coming to terms that my adopted parents hid the truth that they knew my true identity and that I had relatives. My uncle Preston blackmailed them, and they paid him to keep me. I had never doubted my parents' love for me, and this just added to my beliefs.

I struggled to understand why they hid this from me after I reached adulthood. Perhaps they thought I would turn on them. I might have. If they had told me, I would have met my brother under better circumstances, and that could have saved many lives.

I wouldn't have met my birth parents, though. While I hadn't decided if ghosts existed, even with Ruby's insistence they did, I found comfort in coming to the tomb here.

I warmed my hands with the coffee cup as Mr. Hugo sang "Amazing Grace." His deep, rich baritone voice added to the tranquil atmosphere of the cemetery. Soon, tour guides would share the history of the tombs for tourists, snapping photos. For now, Mr. Hugo's singing soothed my heart.

"Thank you. Your voice always calms my nerves," I said when he finished.

"Anytime, my dear. If I don't see you on your way out, happy birthday."

"I hope I'll see you at my party next week," I said.

"Now you better save me a dance at your birthday party."

"Only if your wife isn't dancing with you all night."

"Sorry, but she's hosting her bunco group that night. She wanted to come and finally meet you. One day, I hope."

"Yes, definitely one day." I stood on my tiptoes and kissed Mr. Hugo on the cheek. "Thanks again."

Mr. Hugo hummed a song I didn't recognize as he left me alone with my thoughts. I sat on the step and pulled my jacket tighter around my body. The chill in the air and the cool mausoleum step weren't comfortable. I sipped my coffee, hoping it would warm me up.

But it wasn't my coffee but my cousin, Jasper, that did.

"Happy birthday, Sammy." Dressed in jeans and an olive-green crew-neck sweater, Jasper sat down next to me.

"Hey, there. I didn't expect to see you here."

"Momma wanted me to bring flowers to the tomb. She's busy with Momo and Nora." Jasper placed a vase of pink roses on the ground in front of us.

"That was sweet of her." My eyes welled up. "I'm not sure why I'm so emotional this morning."

"Well, you are an old lady today." Jasper put his arm around me.

"Take that back." I elbowed him in his side. "I'd like to remind you that you are older than me."

"Fine. I take it back." Jasper smiled. "But really, Sammy, this is the first year you've known when your actual birthday is. It's got to be overwhelming."

"Don't get me wrong, I'm glad for the information. I just feel guilty about being happy to know everything about my birth parents. Even though my adopted parents are dead, I still feel guilty." I blew out a deep breath. "But I also am upset that my parents kept this from me."

"It's all right to have mixed emotions. Not everything in this world is black and white."

I wiped the tears from my face. "You're now designated as my therapist."

"Only if you'll be mine." Jasper squeezed me tighter. "We've got each other, Cousin. And don't forget Momma."

"No one can forget your mom." I laughed. "Speaking of her, why did she want you to bring flowers today?"

"She meant to bring them on your actual birthday, but was too busy. Momma thought today was good, too. She knows how much your parents loved you, so she wanted to show them she was thinking of them and you."

My tears started again. "Aunt Charlene can be so thoughtful."

"Don't cry." Jasper reached into his jeans pocket and pulled out a crumpled napkin.

I dotted my eyes. "Thanks. I guess this old lady just needed to cry. But now I need beignets. Care to join me?"

Jasper jumped up and reached his hand out to me. I let him pull me up and into a hug. "Only if you'll let me buy. It is your birthday after all. I assume we're going to Cafe Beignet."

"You know it." I grinned.

I picked up the vase and inhaled the sweet scent of the roses. "Bye, everyone," I said as I placed the vase on the step. I followed Jasper out of the cemetery and toward Cafe Beignet on Royal Street. He didn't need to ask which one, even though there were other locations. The Royal Street location was my favorite, but it sat next to the police station. With a bit of luck, Rob and Christine would be there, and I might get some information about the case. It was my birthday after all.

23

The line was inside the door when we arrived at Cafe Beignet. At times, the line would be out the door and down the sidewalk. After 9 a.m., flocks of tourists would take photos of the tan-colored building with its green-and-white awning and large Cafe Beignet sign. To the left of the entrance, a wrought-iron fence encased the patio. On the other side of the patio was the French Quarter police station, so not only did I want beignets, I hoped Rob and Christine would stop in for coffee.

We ordered at the counter and sat on the patio. I loved sitting here among the lush plants and trees. Green iron tables with matching stools with heart-shaped backs filled the courtyard. Birds fluttered around, hoping to get beignet crumbs. Cats occasionally weaved in and out of the fence in hopes of treats, too. Today, an orange tabby named Bacon sat by a table with a plate of bacon crumbs and a saucer of cream.

Jasper bought our beignets and café au laits for my birthday. Thankfully, he understood my wish to have a low-key birthday and didn't put a candle in one of my beignets.

"That was so good." Jasper finished the last of his three beignets. He brushed a streak of powdered sugar from his jeans.

"Nothing better than a beignet." I had finished my second one. "Well, gumbo, muffulettas, and jambalaya are high on my list, too."

"I agree. I hate to leave you, but I've got to meet Neal this morning for a work meeting," Jasper said.

"Do y'all have house meetings, too?" Jasper and Neal had been roommates for five months. Since they lived and worked together, I checked in now and again on their relationship.

"We should." Jasper rolled his eyes. "His idea of cleaning dishes is leaving them soaking in the sink for days until the crud comes off. I've rewashed tons of dishes."

I wrinkled my nose. "Ew. Doesn't it smell?"

"It's not as pungent as his pile of dirty laundry he keeps right by his bedroom door." Jasper laughed. "Neal isn't a neat freak like me, he says. I'm far from one, according to my mother."

"Speaking of your mom, how is it going with Momo?"

"She loves Momo and Nora. It's been a while since she's felt needed, she told me. I guess me leaving home still bothers her." Jasper rubbed the crescent-shaped scar on his face. Recently, Jasper had been rubbing his scar less, which was a relief because he used to rub it when he felt stressed or worried.

"Remember, you're not responsible for your mother's happiness." I reached over the table and squeezed his hand. "I admire how she's carving her own path after all she's been through."

"You're right. I just hope she has a plan for when Nora passes. I'm afraid she'll feel lost afterwards."

"It sounds like something you need to talk to her about. If you want me to help, I will," I said.

"Thanks. You're the best cousin." Jasper stood up. "I'll give you a heads-up when I'm ready to talk to her. I've got to go. Are you leaving now, too?"

"I'm not in a rush to go to the store. I still have a beignet left to eat."

"And you're hoping Rob and Christine will come by, too." Jasper grinned. "We all know you too well."

"Yes, y'all do." I got up and hugged Jasper. "Thanks for the birthday breakfast."

Jasper left for his meeting, and I stayed at the same table. I did reposition myself so I could see the entrance of the police station. The patio was open to the building, so Rob and Christine would walk into the café this way. If they did at all this morning. I could stay until nine, so I settled into my chair. While waiting, I used my phone to check my emails and texts. All the birthday messages from friends near and far overwhelmed me.

"So you just happen to be here?"

I looked up to find Christine staring at me. "Hey, Christine. I'm enjoying beignets and coffee on my birthday."

Christine's face softened. "That's right. Happy birthday, Sammy."

"Thanks! Where's your partner in..."

"Don't say in crime. It's ridiculous." Christine's serious face returned.

"Sorry. I guess a lot of people say that." I looked past Christine and saw Rob on his phone in front of the station. "It must be your turn to buy coffee and beignets. I see Rob's on his phone."

"Never fails that he gets a call when we're going out for coffee. That man owes me more money than a gambler owes the house on a losing streak." She sighed and took a seat at the table. "Since you're here, let me ask you a question. Did you see any papers around the courtyard when you and Mrs. Townsend found Paige?"

"Only the scrap of paper in Paige's hand. The one I didn't touch," I said.

"Simmer down, Nancy Drew. I'm just asking," Christine said. "Wait, I should call you Miss Marple, since you're older today."

I tried to give her a dirty look, but I laughed along with her. Not that I would tell her, but I loved our banter. Christine presented herself in such a serious manner that her moments of lightness and laughter charmed me.

After I stopped laughing, I asked, "Why are you asking about papers? What was in Paige's hand? It must have been from something important."

"Since it's your birthday, I'll give you a little present, but I need something in return," Christine said.

"Umm, I don't think you're supposed to expect something from the person you give a gift to," I deadpanned, but Christine's stern looked made me rethink my joke. "Fine. I always tell you anything I know."

"You better." Christine smiled. "Let me start by telling you that this paper is from an autopsy report."

"Hollis's autopsy?" I gasped.

"Yes. But we haven't found the rest of it on the Davenport property. Has anyone in the family or Nora Winslow mentioned anything to you?"

I shook my head. "I wonder if Paige was taking it from someone or trying to keep someone from taking it from her."

"We don't know yet. And before you ask, we've ordered a

copy. We'll have to wait a few days because it's not digitized yet. The family can't remember if they had a copy."

"Why would they have the autopsy report?" I asked.

"Legally, family members can have a copy. We searched the rest of Paige's house and didn't find it. There were boxes of records in a storeroom in the outbuilding."

"I wish I had seen something to help you out," I said.

"Me, too." She sighed. "Look who finally joined us. It's your turn to buy today, partner."

Rob stood by the table now. "Sorry, Christine, no time today. We just got a call about a death that relates to our case."

Goose bumps popped up on my arms. "It's not Nora, is it?"

Rob rested his hand on my shoulder. "No, Sammy, it's not Nora or Momo. Don't worry."

"Who is it?" Christine jumped out of her chair and took her keys out of her pocket. "And where are we going?"

"It was Paige's boyfriend. Tate King was found dead at his home just thirty minutes ago."

24

———————

Tate King was dead? But I just saw him last night. What happened after Sissy and I left the bar?

"Sammy, why did the blood rush out of your face? What do you know?" Christine sat back down at the table. Rob borrowed a chair from another table and sat on the other side of me.

"Did you know Tate King? You never said you did." Rob's voice carried a tone of accusation.

"I met him last night," I squeaked.

"Sissy mentioned that you two tried out Randall's last night. Let me guess: that's Tate King's hangout?" Rob said.

"Rob, give her a break. We were about to talk about what Sammy knew about the case when you came over," Christine said.

My face must have been pale enough for Christine to defend me. Knowing she trusted me to be truthful and open comforted me.

"Fine. I should've realized something was going on when you two went to a place other than The Gas Light,"

Rob muttered, his frown lingering, though his voice held less anger.

"I found out that Tate hangs out at Randall's, so we went to ask him about Paige." And other things, but I didn't need to tell them that.

"Tell us everything you talked about." Rob pulled out his pen and notebook from his gray suit jacket.

I recounted the conversation, ending with our run-in with Winston. Rob and Christine were so good at keeping blank faces as I spoke. Their turn arrived.

"Did he seem depressed? Had he been drinking heavily?" Christine said.

"He was brokenhearted, and I believe he was drinking nonalcoholic beer. Tammy, the bartender at Randall's, will know," I said. "You don't think he took his own life, do you?"

"We know nothing yet. But it's a pertinent question, considering Paige's recent death," Christine said.

"You mentioned Winston Briggs came into the bar as you were leaving. Had he scheduled a meeting, or was it like a casual drop-in, like you and Sissy?" Rob said.

"I'd say arranged. Tate said he needed to be alone and then checked his watch. I'm assuming now he was waiting for Winston," I said.

Christine pushed her chair back and stood up. She towered over me. "We need to get to the scene. But just a reminder not to speak with Tammy or Winston about this case."

"Especially before we do." Rob stooped and kissed me on the cheek. "Let us do our job, and you do your best to have a great birthday."

"What he said," Christine said.

"I will."

Rob and Christine rushed out, and I lingered in my seat for a few more minutes. I pushed my coffee and the rest of my beignets to the side. The thought of finishing made me nauseous. Before heading to the shop, I needed a moment to gather myself. Why was Tate dead? Was it suicide or murder?

"Oh, dear. This isn't good news at all." Andrew hugged me after I explained what I learned last night from Tate and how he was dead this morning. "Could it have been an accident?"

"Doesn't it seem a bit of a coincidence?" I walked through the shop and opened the office door. "He suggested he knew the family's secrets, was seen talking to a journalist, and then died?"

"Yes, it does. But until you learn more from Rob and Christine, you need to put it aside for now." Andrew took my coat from me and hung it on the coatrack.

"I will, I promise," I said. "It's going to be a busy day, and I don't want to miss out on any sales."

"I'm never worried about your commitment to our business, my dear. You're incredibly good at staying focused on what needs to be done." Andrew's warm smile confirmed his words.

"Thanks. Let's get those sales." I closed the office door and cleared my head of thoughts of Paige's, and now Tate's, deaths.

Just ten minutes before we would open the shop, a series of knocks shook the front door. I peered out the window to find last night's partner in crime. Sissy, with her long blonde locks flying around her face and her knuckles rapping on the door, appeared irritable.

"Sissy, what's wrong?" I asked after I ushered her inside.

"What's wrong? You didn't text me this morning. That's what's wrong!" She brushed the hair off her flushed face.

"I'm so sorry. I rushed from Cafe Beignet to the shop." My face felt as warm as Sissy's looked. "Did Rob call you?"

"Yes, he did. And you can imagine how that went." Sissy leaned up against the display table and sales desk. "I was so shocked to hear that Tate was dead. That poor man."

I took a place next to Sissy. "I know, and I'm sorry it was Rob that told you and not me."

Sissy rested her head on my shoulder. "Sorry to rush in here like it was the opening day for king cakes at Manny Randazzo's."

"I'll remember that when we go for king cake next year." I said.

"Are you two ladies done apologizing to each other?" Andrew had left the room and returned with two mugs of coffee.

"Sorry, Dad," Sissy and I said in unison.

"Your shtick is getting old." Andrew handed us our mugs. "And don't say I am, too, or I'll take away your cell phones."

"No, not that!" Sissy laughed. "Sorry to interrupt your morning, Andrew."

"We have about ten minutes before we open, so why don't you two go into the office and catch up," Andrew said.

"Thanks. I promise I'll be quick." I led Sissy back to the office and closed the door.

"I'll make this short and sweet." Sissy sat down in a chair. "Rob said you told him about our conversation with

Tate and that Winston showed up. Which turned out to be quite interesting to them because Winston found Tate's body."

"He did?" I dropped into the chair behind the desk and let that information sink in.

"Yes, but that's all I got from him about that. But pull up Winston's blog on your laptop."

I did as Sissy said and went to Winston's Whispers website. The first post said,

"Breaking News! Your intrepid reporter, Winston Briggs, discovered the body of Tate King this morning. I can't reveal too much yet, but I can tell you that the police are investigating his death.

Tate King was the current or ex-boyfriend, depending on who you speak to, of murder victim Paige Townsend. I had an exclusive interview set for this morning with Mr. King. Did the information he had contribute to his death? Did he kill himself? Was he murdered? Sign up for alerts to receive my latest information on this sad and mysterious crime."

"Now, that's interesting, considering we saw him with Tate last night. Why didn't he do the interview then? They could have spoken privately at one of the tables in the corner," I said.

"Maybe Tate refused and Winston killed him as revenge," Sissy said.

"Come on, Sissy. Winston is a jerk, but would he murder someone for a story?"

"Probably not. But it'll be interesting to hear the actual story from him. But I can't track him down today." Sissy sat up from her chair.

"No, you shouldn't. It'll annoy Rob and Christine."

"Oh, yeah, that, too." Sissy giggled. "But actually, I signed up to help wrap gifts for the kids at the hospital today."

"You're so thoughtful. Hold it, are you good at wrapping gifts? I only ask because I'm horrible at it." From using too much or too little paper to tying crooked bows, I didn't have the knack for it.

"It's one of my many talents." Sissy opened the office door. "Andrew, I'm returning Sammy to you. But I need to buy a dozen kids' books for the hospital party."

"You don't need to do that to make up for your slight disruption." Andrew put his arm around Sissy. "But let me take you to the children's section."

I opened the shop as Andrew and Sissy looked over books. A line of customers filed into Lagniappe Books, with smiles on their faces. I had a busy morning visiting my family's grave, eating beignets with Jasper, followed by the news of Tate's death from Rob and Christine. A day of helping customers find the perfect books would keep my mind on books and not murders.

25

———

"**C**onnor, can you grab my coat? I'm almost ready."

"Sammy, you said that ten minutes ago." Connor poked his head into my bedroom. "Don't worry, we have plenty of time. Wow, you look amazing."

Work was busy, as expected, and more birthday messages arrived throughout the day. Momo and Nora called together and sang a very off-key version of "Happy Birthday." Just hearing their voices together in such a joyful tone was one of the best presents I had received.

I couldn't deny that dinner tonight was another wonderful present. Connor, Libby, and William were taking me to Antoine's Restaurant. Ever since I read Frances Parkinson Keyes's book, *Dinner at Antoine's*, I wanted to go there. I love going to places I read about in books, especially if it's a mystery.

"Thank you. Sissy helped me pick out this dress." I did a twirl, making the skirt flutter. "She wanted me to buy it in purple, but I loved it in black."

Connor picked up me by the waist and spun me around.

"You wear black all the time. One day we'll get you in bright New Orleans colors."

"You and Sissy can keep trying."

"We both like a challenge." Connor grinned. "Let's head to the restaurant now. Mom and Dad are meeting us there."

The walk to Antoine's Restaurant took a little longer than we planned. Many of the musicians playing on the street corners were friends of Connor's. We stopped to listen to one band and ended up dancing to their rendition of "It's a Wonderful World." The bustling crowd faded as we danced. My heart skipped a beat as Connor and I danced. His powerful arms embraced me as we swayed to the soulful music. We sang along to the song, lost in our own world. Nothing is more romantic than dancing with your boyfriend in the streets of the French Quarter.

We arrived at Antoine's at the same time as Libby and William. We were all dressed up for the evening. William and Connor wore a jacket and tie, and Libby and I were in fancy dresses.

"Look at you two! Such a beautiful couple." Libby hugged me, then Connor. "And happy birthday, Sammy. We're so happy we can celebrate together."

William shook Connor's hand and kissed me on the cheek. "Happy birthday, dear Samantha. I hope you're ready for a delicious meal. This is one of my favorite restaurants in the Quarter."

"I definitely am," I said.

As we walked from the main dining room to the back one, my mouth starting watering from all the dishes. I recognized the oysters Rockefeller, a dish originating here. At another table, a server made café brûlot, table side. Blue flames followed the trail of orange peel studded with cloves, held over a silver punch bowl. A mix of brandy, triple sec, and chicory coffee made for a delightful scent as we passed by.

We sat in the Large Annex, previously a stable block. Photos of famous guests lined the red walls lit by the chandeliers throughout the room. Our server came over and we ordered cocktails, appetizers, and entrées. Our drinks came out first: two Sazerac and two French 75s.

"You're not having a Pimm's Cup? You must be growing up." William's laugh sounded just like Connor's.

"No, I'm trying to expand my cocktail repertoire. I've never had one." From the first sip of my drink, I discovered what I had been missing. The light fizz of the champagne blended well with gin, sugar, and lemon. "Is this what my thirties will hold? Picking new cocktails. If so, I'll enjoy getting old."

"You are too funny and too cute." Libby lifted her French 75. "Let's cheer to Sammy's birthday. We are so happy to have you in our lives."

William raised his glass. "Yes, we are."

"Hear! Hear!" Connor held his glass with one hand and held my hand in the other. "You make my life full of love and mystery. Don't stop."

"I'm so thankful to have y'all in my life. New Orleans wouldn't be what it is without your love." My cheeks hurt from smiling so wide and so much.

Over our appetizers, we caught up on the past week. I did most of the talking, so all three of them knew about Paige's death and now Tate's.

"Poor Lydia. She's had so many bumps in her life," Libby said.

"I didn't realize you knew her," I said.

"Not well, but we were on an arts committee together. She offered to donate quite a large sum of money, but then backed out. She said there was a hiccup in her finances and never returned to the group," Libby said.

"I remember that. Lydia seemed so invested in the project." William took another oysters Rockefeller. The spinach and cheese were a rich complement to the briny oyster. I liked them, but not as much as the soufflé potatoes. The fried potatoes were light and fluffy and the béarnaise sauce added a richness to the appetizer.

"Yes, she did." Libby shook her head at Connor as he tried to sneak in another oyster. "The rumor was she didn't have access to the money she offered. Apparently, she expected her daughter to use her trust fund money for the cause. Paige said no and that this wasn't the first time."

"I heard a similar story from Gideon Pearce," I said. "It seems Paige's financial situation was better than her mother's."

"I never worked with the Davenport family, but there were rumors that dissolving Davenport Oil put a strain on the sisters' finances," William said. "The company employed both their husbands, but neither of them ever replaced Mr. Davenport."

"He expected his son Hollis to take charge, according to Nora," I said.

"That was the rumor, but Hollis's untimely death changed the trajectory of the company," William said.

"Oh, I remember this story. Mr. Davenport sold the business and later died. His wife died soon after." Libby reached for Connor's hand. "Losing a child is unimaginable."

"You've got me always, Momma." Connor squeezed his mother's hand. "At least until you give me the recipe for your hummingbird cake."

Connor's joke lightened the mood, and we had a joyful evening as we ate our meal. But I couldn't help but wonder about the Davenport family's financial situation. Lydia appeared to have money problems. I suspected Emerson had issues, too, by the way he was looking for business, even the day after his cousin's death. Was Dorothy in the same situation as her sister? I had more questions than answers tonight.

"Are you sure you don't want café brûlot?" William asked after we ordered dessert.

"Yes, thanks. I don't know how I'm going to finish my crème brûlée," I said.

"I'd rather have dessert than café brûlot." Connor patted his stomach. "Anyway, we're going to The Gas Light after this. If I don't bring Sammy there, I will feel the wrath of our friends."

"While we're waiting for dessert, you should take Sammy around the restaurant, Connor. I'm sure she wants to see the 1840s' room. It was in the book *Dinner at Antoine's*," William said.

"Take your picture in front of the Mystery Room. It seems appropriate for our amateur detective." Libby laughed.

"Let's go." I had to stop myself from jumping out of my seat. I didn't want to embarrass myself in front of Libby and William or the other guests.

Connor took me to see the private dining rooms on the first floor. All the rooms, except the Mystery Room, were full of private parties, so I could only see a glimpse inside. The names of three Mardi Gras krewes, and their pictures and Mardi Gras paraphernalia, decorated three of the rooms. Brightly painted walls and elegant china and crystal added to the charm of the rooms. Connor promised to bring me back to see them and also to eat more oysters.

The Mystery room was empty, so we could explore it at our own leisure. Framed alcohol advertisements, menus, newspaper articles, and photographs lined the walls. I could have stayed here for hours pouring over all the history in this room alone. But I pulled myself away to join Connor at the entrance to the room.

"Let me take a photo of you in the doorway," Connor said. The room's name was over the door's archway, so Connor insisted I stand there.

"Do you want a serious pose or a smiling one?" I asked Connor as he snapped photos with his cell phone.

"Both. One for your Facebook profile and another for your detective license."

"Funny. Very funny." I put my hands on my hips and smiled. "Now you can tell me why it's called the Mystery Room."

"The story goes that during Prohibition, customers would use a door in the ladies' room to come in here. They'd get their alcohol in a coffee cup. And when someone asked what they were drinking, they'd say, 'It's a mystery to me.' Cool story, huh?"

"A very New Orleans story." I laughed. "I love that I'm still learning all these quirky stories after being here for almost a year."

"Darling, there are more strange things to learn about the city." Connor came over to me and we snapped a selfie. "And speaking of strange, we better eat our dessert and head to The Gas Light."

"Agreed. We don't want our absence to be a mystery."

"Yep. You might be the group's amateur sleuth, but

they'd do anything to find you." Connor and I kissed until a soft cough interrupted us.

"Sorry, we got distracted." My face felt warm, but Connor just laughed.

"You're fine, miss. Your family just asked me to look for you. Dessert is ready." Our server smiled and waited for us to go back to the dining room first.

Connor and I returned to our table to find William and Libby grinning as we returned.

"We thought you lost your way. If you didn't come back, your desserts were ours." Libby winked.

While I loved dessert, I would have given it up if the Mystery Room had given me answers to Hollis's and Paige's deaths.

26

"What is Winston doing here?" Connor grumbled as we got closer to The Gas Light. Winston's fedora bounced off his head as he paced back and forth in front of the bar door. Even in the faint gaslight, the strained muscles in his neck and face were evident. His eyes widened when he noticed Connor and me.

"Sammy, there you are! I need to talk to you." Winston rushed up to us. "You heard about Tate King, right?"

"Yes, I did. Are you all right after finding him?" I asked.

"Umm, yeah. Thanks for asking," Winston stammered. "No one has asked me that."

"Sammy cares about people—unlike you," Connor snarled.

"Let's be civil, both of you," I said before Winston snapped back at Connor. Winston wasn't my favorite person, but knowing firsthand what it's like to find a body, I showed him some kindness. The nicer I was, the more information I might get.

"You're right. Winston, do you want to join us inside?" Connor put his arm around my waist. "It's Sammy's birthday, so we're meeting our friends."

"Umm, no thanks. Can I just talk to you for a minute, Sammy? I promise it won't be long," Winston said. "Connor, you can stay."

Connor looked at me for the answer. I adored he didn't feel the need to act like a knight in shining armor. He was sure I could deal with the situation.

"We can talk out here for a few minutes. Connor, I'll be in, in a soon. Tell the group I am really here."

"Will do." Connor entered The Gas Light. The warmth and cheerful sounds from inside made me want to follow him in. But I needed to hear what Winston had to say.

"Okay, let's talk. It's cold out here." I pulled my coat tighter around me.

"Do you want my jacket?" Winston asked.

"No, thanks. So we both have questions, but I'm going to start," I said.

"Seeing it's your birthday, fine." Winston dramatically sighed.

"Thanks for being so generous." I rolled my eyes. Winston just couldn't help himself. "Anyway, I suppose you interviewed Tate last night about Paige's death. What did he say?"

"Probably the same thing he said to you. I'm shocked that you got to him before me."

"Focus, Winston. Yes, he told me he suspected Paige's family had something to do with her death." I decided not to mention anything about Nora and Hollis's story. The last thing she needed was her name splashed on Winston's blog.

"Did he give you any specific details? He alluded to

things, but didn't give me any useful information." Winston stepped to the side to let a couple go into the bar.

"No, just that he didn't trust them. I'm surprised he didn't tell you more," I said.

"He said he'd tell me tomorrow. That's why I visited his apartment this morning. I wanted to catch up before he, uh, went out."

I stared at Winston to make him uncomfortable. He must be holding back. Granted, I was, too, but having been in enough staring contests with Nubi, I would outlast him. Also, Winston didn't like silence. He preferred to listen to his own voice.

"Fine, I'll tell you the truth." Winston stepped closer to me, so much so that I smelled his pungent cologne. "I sometimes pay people for their time, especially if they have fantastic dirt, or rather information."

"I can't say I'm surprised. You are tenacious, and I wondered how you got some interviews you've had." I gave him my best disapproving frown. "Did you pay Tate that night?"

"I offered him money, and he seemed interested. But when I got back from the restroom, he said he wanted to think about it," Winston said. "He denied he was pushing for more money, but he wouldn't make eye contact with me. I think he looked for another source of money. But no one else would pay him what I could."

"That's not something to brag about, Winston."

"Fine. But I believe he thought he could get more money for whatever info he had on Paige's family. If he wasn't going to another journalist, he probably went to Paige's mother," Winston said.

Winston must not have known that Lydia had financial troubles. Tate could have tried to blackmail her, but

Dorothy and Emerson were better candidates. Or perhaps he went to all three?

"Did you tell this to the police? Rob and Christine need to know." Like Connor, Christina and Rob had little patience for Winston, but it wouldn't keep them from talking to him.

"I did. And I asked for police protection, but they said no."

"Oh." I rubbed my hands together to keep warm. "That must mean whatever you saw at Tate's apartment scared you into thinking he was murdered."

"Exactly!" Winston let out a huge breath. "His front door was open when I got there around eight. At first, I thought he was drunk. There were beer bottles around him on his couch. But when he didn't respond to my yelling, I went over to him."

"It's all right. Take your time." Winston was visibly shaking, but he calmed himself quickly.

"I'm fine. So I checked for a pulse and then called the police," Winston said. "He had been dead for a while, so hopefully they've taken me off their suspect list. Honestly, I can't take that again."

"I can understand that." Having been on the police suspect list before, I sympathized with his fears.

"Did you notice if the beer was nonalcoholic?" I said.

"Actually it was nonalcoholic beer. Yuck. Oh, you're asking because Tate said he was a recovering alcoholic. Besides the beer, there were some pills scattered on his coffee table."

Did my conversation, and then Winston's, set Tate off? Did he take pills with his beer? I wondered what kind of pills they were.

"Sammy, are you okay? Listen, if Tate was as depressed

as I think he was, nothing we said made a difference," Winston said as if he had read my mind.

"So you think he killed himself?"

"Maybe, but it seems awfully suspicious that he dies after putting me off. Unless he did murder Paige and the guilt got to him."

"Suspicious is the right word," I said.

That's all I wanted to say to Winston. I didn't want him exploiting Tate's death for his own gain, especially while the police were investigating. If someone murdered him, it had to be the same person who killed Paige. What did the both of them know?

"Are you sure you don't want to come inside?" I asked Winston.

"You're just being polite. You know your friends and your boyfriend don't want me to join your celebration."

While it was true, I tried to be polite. Especially since he shared his information, and he said he was worried about his safety. But if Rob and Christine weren't concerned, he should be all right.

"Stay safe and keep me in the loop if you learn anything else," I said.

"Same goes for you." Winston tipped his hat and walked away. After a few steps, he turned around and said, "Happy birthday, Sammy."

I waved goodbye and headed into The Gas Light. Shouts of "Happy Birthday" almost made me turn back around.

"Thanks, everyone," I mumbled as I made my way to the bar. I glared at Sissy, Jasper, Neal, and Connor, who were standing up at a table in the back. By their grins, I knew they had talked everyone into wishing me a happy birthday.

Before I went back to scold them, I found a seat at the far end of the bar. "Hey, Rose."

"Sammy, happy birthday." Rose smiled. "I swear I had nothing to do with everyone shouting at you."

"Thanks. Have you talked to Tammy?" I asked.

"I called her after I saw the news about Tate." Rose put down the glass she had been drying. "She's shocked and confused. Tate seemed fine to her when he left last night. Well, as fine as you would be if your girlfriend had been murdered, and you were accused of it."

"He was the same when we left. I just talked to Winston, and he said Tate cut their interview off abruptly. Tate said he'd continue it today, but he was dead when Winston found him."

"That explains why Winston came and left in one fell swoop. He wanted to talk to you," Rose said.

"Yes, we exchanged a little information. More him than me. Being accused of murder, earlier this month, he's scared."

"I would be, too. Even if I hadn't been accused of poisoning my former college professor," Rose spoke softly.

"Me, too."

"Hold it. I thought Tate's death was accidental, or he took his own life," Rose said.

"Winston told me it's now a suspicious death, according to his inside source at the police department," I said.

"What do your inside sources say?" Rose raised her eyebrows.

"I assume you mean Rob and Christine. But don't let them know you called them that." I looked around the bar to double-check that they hadn't come in when I wasn't looking.

"Sammy, I'm a bartender. My lips are sealed." Rose smiled.

"Thanks. But I haven't heard anything or even seen them since this morning," I said.

"I'm sure we'll find out sooner rather than later what happened to Tate and to Paige."

"That would be the best birthday gift," I said. And it would be a relief for Momo and Nora, especially.

"Do you want a Pimm's Cup? Or would you like a piña colada? Apparently, it's on the drink list now." Rose pointed over to Aunt Charlene and Terry, who sat next to each other at the table.

By the bemused looks from Connor, Neal, Sissy, and Jasper, the twosome were having a good time. Jasper caught my eyes, and we smiled at each other. In the midst of all the sadness of Nora's illness and now two murders, I was glad to see some happiness growing between two people.

"I don't like piña coladas, and I wouldn't want you to have to use the blender. I'm still embarrassed by everyone singing happy birthday to me," I said.

"This is what you get when you have your own neighborhood bar." Rose laughed. "Now go sit down and I'll bring your drink to you. A Pimm's Cup, I promise."

"There's my girl!" Aunt Charlene jumped up and hugged me when I reached the table.

"I wanted to bring a cake and presents here, but we'll do it at your party. You don't mind, do you?" she asked.

"That sounds great, Aunt Charlene," I said.

"Wonderful!" She turned to Terry, and they started talking about fishing. My aunt had a lot more interests than I realized.

"You can thank me for keeping Momma from turning tonight into another party," Jasper whispered in my ear. An Elvis impersonator might have walked in singing just to you."

"I owe you. Once again," I whispered back.

"Just remember this when my birthday comes up. I had an Elvis impersonator for my tenth birthday, and once was enough."

"It's a deal," I promised.

The conversation around the table offered a welcome change from talk of murders. Terry and Aunt Charlene joined us from time to time, but they mostly kept talking to each other. I couldn't help but wonder if Connor, Sissy, Neal, and Jasper had agreed to talk about anything but Tate and Paige. After I finished my drink, I was ready to call it a night.

"Hey, y'all, thanks for the birthday celebration. But I need to go home since tomorrow's another workday." I tried to stifle a yawn but didn't succeed.

Everyone agreed to leave together except Aunt Charlene and Terry.

"I'll walk Miss Charlene home. We promised Jimmy and Bob at least one round of poker," Terry said. "They're trying to earn their peanuts back. And their pride. They didn't see you coming, Charlene."

"I have to thank Momo for her tips. Now, she's the real deal." Aunt Charlene blushed. "Oh, Sammy, I almost forgot! Paige's family is holding a memorial service for her tomorrow afternoon. Nora hoped you could come along with us. Momo and I are going with her."

"Anything for Nora," I said. "Where and what time?"

"In the courtyard at the Davenport house at five. Could you come to Momo's first? We might need help to get Nora into her wheelchair," Aunt Charlene said. "Poor thing has been exhausted lately."

"I'm glad to help." I hugged Aunt Charlene and Terry before following my friends out of the bar.

I'd do anything to help Nora. She hadn't made it to the house the day Paige died. Could she do it this time? I hoped so because I believed there had to be more to learn there. Tomorrow, I needed to find out more about Paige and her family. Would tomorrow be the day all the pieces came together to find out the truth about Hollis and Paige?

27

───────

"There she is! I haven't seen you all week, Sammy!" Francesca Fortuna welcomed me with open arms into her shop, Frankie's Groceries. Somehow Frankie contained her energy in her barely five foot tall body. Whatever she and Momo did to be so vibrant in their later years, I needed them to share with me.

"Sorry, it's been a crazy week," I said after I caught my breath from Frankie's bear hug. "I ran out of coffee creamer and I can't live without that."

I finished my last bottle of coffee creamer this morning, so I popped into Frankie's before I headed off to work. I missed chatting with her about her life and the latest gossip. Not that Frankie called it gossip. She didn't want to be called a tattle-tale, so she called herself the local storyteller. Frankie wasn't wrong. I could listen to her for hours about her childhood, to the origin of New Orleans legends and lore.

Today I had little time since I needed to get to work. Andrew offered to close the store alone so I could attend the memorial with Nora and Momo early this evening. Since I needed creamer at home, I decided I should pick up lunch for Andrew and me.

Frankie's Groceries offered locals all the packaged foods and sundries imaginable, in addition to the best homemade Italian and Southern dishes. There was no other corner store in the Quarter that offered the variety of prepared meals that Frankie did.

"I've heard from Momo about all the activity at her house." Frankie rubbed her hands on her apron. "Your aunt came in to restock Momo's shelves. Charlene is a hoot! And such a big help to Momo."

"She is all that." I laughed. "What do you suggest for lunch today, Frankie?" I perused the deli counter filled with fried chicken, pasta bolognese, mac 'n' cheese, and dirty rice. Frankie also offered made to order sandwiches like muffulettas and po' boys.

Before she answered, her grandson and namesake, Frank, came out from the kitchen.

"Hey, Sammy! I'd get the fried chicken if I were you." Frank's eyes twinkled just like his grandmother's.

"Let me guess. You made the fried chicken today," I said.

Frankie was letting Frank cook more now that she approved of his recipes. Over the past month, Frank had made a few changes to the family's recipes. Adding home-made bacon salt to the fried chicken was his best so far.

"I did. And I also recommend the dirty rice. Nonna cooked it." Frank put his arm around his grandmother.

"Can I have two plates with the rice, fried chicken, and coleslaw?" I said.

"Coming right up!" Frankie raised the hinged countertop by the deli and placed it back down.

"Hey, Sammy. Can I ask you about cookbooks? Do they

sell well? I keep telling Nonna we need to make one of all her recipes," Frank asked.

As Frankie put together my lunches, Frank and I talked about cookbooks. I loved the idea. It would sell well in the shop and in Lagniappe Books. I would buy a copy. Not for me to use, but for Connor. I felt so lucky to have a boyfriend who was a better cook than I.

While we were finishing up our chat, the door opened. I did a double take. Emerson, dressed in a light gray suit with even darker circles under his eyes, trudged into the store.

"Oh, Emerson! You look exhausted." Frankie came out from behind the counter and rushed toward him. Emerson must be used to Frankie's hugs as he braced himself. Instead, Frankie reached up with both hands and pulled his face closer to hers.

"Emerson, you need to take care of yourself. Not just for yourself, but for your momma and aunt." Frankie tsk tsked as she studied his face. She released him and Emerson narrowly avoided knocking over a potato chip display.

"I know. I know. There's been a lot to do." Emerson sighed. "Including picking up the food and drinks for the memorial service. I told her it was too early, but you understand my mom's obsession with everything being in order."

"That I do." Frankie laughed. "Come to the kitchen, and I'll show you everything I've done."

"Thanks, Miss Frankie. And mom wanted me to remind you that you said you could come early to warm up the food," Emerson said.

"Well, of course I am!" Frankie put her hands on her hips.

"Sorry. Mom's very anxious. If I didn't say something, she'd ask you if I had. Things can snowball with her." Emerson's face turned red.

"I understand about moms. And grandmothers." Frank laughed.

"Hey, Frank. I didn't realize you were here. Or you." Emerson furrowed his brow. "I just run into you in the strangest places, Samantha."

Meeting at a local grocery store didn't seem strange to me. By his face and his stiff posture, I decided not to argue with him. Instead I asked, "How are you Emerson? And your family?"

"Hanging in there. Thank you for asking." His tone was softer, but the tension in his body hadn't dissipated. "Miss Frankie, may we go to the kitchen now?"

Frankie headed toward the kitchen, with Emerson following.

"I put aside that beer you bought the other day. I'm so proud of you for taking care of yourself." Frankie patted Emerson on the arm.

"What? Oh, that." Emerson rubbed the back of his neck. "Thanks."

As soon as the kitchen door closed, Frank said, "You're dying to know what Nonna meant, aren't you?"

"No." I felt flushed. Did everyone think I was nosy?

"Sammy, don't be embarrassed. I bet you're looking into Paige Townsend's death. We all know how close you and Momo are." Frank grinned.

"Fine. I admit I'm nosy," I said.

"And you're looking into Paige's death?"

"Yes, that too."

"Well, then, I'll tell you what I saw, since Nonna won't tell you," Frank said. "She gossips, but when it comes to someone kicking their drinking habit, she won't. Her grandfather was an alcoholic, and she always tries to help anyone who is quitting."

"Emerson is an alcoholic?"

"Nonna didn't say, but she told me to order more of the nonalcoholic beer since more people were buying it," Frank said.

"And by people you mean Emerson," I said.

"Yes, but you didn't hear it from me," Frank put a finger to his lips.

"Understood. Do you remember when this was?"

Frank tapped his foot. "I'm pretty sure it was Friday. I can look it up if you want. He puts everything on the family's account."

As much as I wanted to ask him to do that, I didn't. Instead, I did the right thing. "You need to call Rob and Christine about this. It might be nothing, but it could be important."

"That's the night Tate died." It was as if a lightbulb went off in Frank's head. "I heard Tate overdosed. You think he drank beer with Emerson?"

"I don't know, but it's worth looking into," I said.

"I'll call them after Emerson leaves. You think it's OK if I don't tell Nonna about it now? I don't want her to worry about this while she's at the memorial."

"That sounds like the right thing to do." I believed it. Not only was Frankie going to the service to pay her respects to the family, but to support Momo.

"Thanks, Sammy. Let me ring up your food before I have to help Nonna and Emerson."

As much as I wanted to stay and try to chat with Emerson, I needed to go to work. Hopefully, I'd have time to talk with him at the memorial service. Had he given up drinking? Or was the pressure of Paige's death getting to him? Or was he feeling guilty?

28

When I arrived at Momo's house, the women were waiting for me. They sat in the kitchen, each with a mug of steaming tea in front of them. All three women wore black: Aunt Charlene and Nora in dresses and Momo in a pantsuit. The atmosphere was heavy with sadness, and Nora's expression reflected a deeper despair. She wrung her hands as she stared down at her tea.

"Hello, everyone." I stood in the doorway.

"We're so glad you're here. Let me go get Nora's wheelchair." Momo jumped out of her chair.

"Momo, you have on two different black shoes," I whispered as she passed me in the doorway.

She looked down at her feet, and a flush crept over her cheeks. "So I have. At least I got the right color. I'll go change first. Thanks, Sammy."

"She's been so disorganized this week," Nora said. "I know it's the stress of taking care of me and Paige's death. Well, and now Tate's death."

"Honey, it's not you. She'd be in worse shape worrying

about you in a cold hospital room." Aunt Charlene grabbed Nora's walker from the corner of the kitchen and put it by her. "Do you want to freshen up before we leave?"

"Yes, I do." Nora took hold of her walker with shaky hands. I almost offered to help, but I remembered Aunt Charlene's words to let her do it herself.

When Nora's bedroom door opened and closed, Aunt Charlene sighed. "Nora feels guilty about everything right now. Have you had any luck finding out what happened to Hollis?"

I shook my head.

"Don't worry, honey. You'll figure it out," Aunt Charlene said.

"Thanks. What's going on with Momo? Is she getting more forgetful?"

"She mixes things up. I was worried she was heading for dementia, but I overheard her talking to her doctor. He told her it sounded like stress and that she was doing too much."

I must get my eavesdropping skills from Aunt Charlene. In this case, I was glad she listened in. "That's good to know. This is a big house for one person and one cat."

Lady Clementine looked up from her spot on a kitchen chair but went right back to sleep.

"It really is, and she's just having a hard time keeping track of what she needs. She went to the store the other day and bought salt instead of sugar. I'm trying to get the kitchen streamlined so she can find things easier," Aunt Charlene said.

"Thank you for being so kind to Momo and Nora."

"It's good for me, too. And I get to stay longer here with my favorite niece."

"Hold it, aren't I your only niece?" I laughed.

"Yes, but you're still my favorite," Aunt Charlene said. "Let's get going."

"Are you ready, Nora?" I asked as we approached the Davenport home.

Nora had been silent the whole way here. Unlike our last trip around the Quarter, she didn't say a word or smile at any of the people or landmarks. We were on our way to a solemn event, but I had hoped she'd find some joy on the way there.

"Yes, I am." Her powerful voice started us. Momo and Charlene gave each other a surprised look. "But I doubt I can walk. Can someone push me into the courtyard?"

"Of course I will. Let's do this, honey." Aunt Charlene charged ahead first, pushing Nora to a man standing at the courtyard gate. He checked a list and then let them in. Having security seemed a bit much, but then again, the media or true crime fans might try to sneak inside.

"I'm not sure if this is the best thing for Nora, but she insisted." Momo threaded her arm through mine. "I told her we could leave at anytime."

"Nora's health is declining, isn't it?" I said.

Momo nodded, and her eyes filled with tears.

"I'm so sorry. It will be hard to lose her."

"I've lost many people over my lifetime, but this one feels different." Momo grasped my arm tighter. "If she doesn't have any resolution about Hollis's and Paige's deaths before she dies..."

"It's all right." I handed Momo a tissue from my purse. "Rob and Christine are working hard."

"And so are you, right?" she pleaded.

"Yes, I am. I hope we'll find some answers at the service. We should go inside before Aunt Charlene rearranges the seats."

Momo dabbed her eyes with the tissue and then chuckled. "If anyone would, it would be Charlene."

We entered the courtyard and found Nora and Aunt Charlene speaking with Dorothy. Her black dress was loose, as if she had shed weight quickly. Which, by the gauntness of her face, it seemed the case.

"Momo, thank you for coming." Dorothy kissed her on the cheek. She reached her hand out to me. "Thank you, Samantha as well. The family appreciates everyone's kindness."

"We wanted to pay our respects to Paige. She really was a special woman," Momo said.

"Indeed. Now if you'll excuse me, I must greet the other guests. Lydia hasn't come out yet to help." Dorothy beelined to the next guests entering the courtyard.

"How can she be angry at Lydia in a moment like this?" Nora fumed. "She's lost her daughter, and now she's supposed to be the perfect hostess. Dorothy always berated her sister. As the oldest, Dorothy always believed she was in control."

"Nothing's changed," Momo said dryly. "If Lydia doesn't come out soon, Dorothy might drag her out. Or worse, make Emerson do it. He has less tact than she does."

"It's all about the family's reputation." Nora sighed. "It was such a burden to Hollis."

Nora looked toward the guesthouse in the back. For a moment, a lightness crossed her face. Wonderful memories must be coming back to her. "Could we go closer to the water fountain, please?"

"Yes, darling. I'll move you there." Aunt Charlene

pushed Nora's wheelchair a few feet, then came back to Momo and me.

"Funerals are the best place to find out the truth, or at least someone's version of it. I'll stay with Nora, and you two should mingle. If you just happen to overhear some news, so be it." Aunt Charlene shooed us off.

"Your aunt amazes me every day. She seems like just a sweet Southern woman, but then she spouts off comments like that." Momo beamed at Aunt Charlene. "And she's a ruthless poker player, too. I'm going to miss her when she goes back to Mississippi."

With that, Momo wandered over to a group of women who welcomed her with open arms. This visit could be good for Momo, too. She had spent most of her time at home over the months. An outing, albeit a memorial service, would get her out into the community again.

I spotted Emerson by the guesthouse with two people I hadn't expected to be here: Rob and Christine. Trying to stay out of their sight lines, I strolled over toward them. I pretended to examine the vines on the courtyard walls as I listened.

"I told you, I was home all night. Tate King is the last person I wanted to see after Paige's death. There's no way I'd be at his house," Emerson huffed. "Why are you here at Paige's service? This couldn't wait until later?"

"We just needed to verify your alibis, Mr. Merritt. Your mother and aunt could not confirm you were home the night of Paige's death nor Tate's," Christine said.

"Of course they wouldn't. I'm not a teenager who has to check in with his mother," Emerson snapped. "Didn't Tate kill himself? That's the rumor in the Quarter. It makes more sense than me murdering him. Tate killed Paige and then himself. Case closed."

"If only it were that simple." Rob's voice was calm and even-keeled. "We also wanted to ask if you knew of any mutual friends of your cousin's and Tate's."

"No," Emerson scoffed. "We led separate and very different lives."

"You weren't her financial advisor, at least?" Christine asked.

"No, she kept her precious trust fund to herself. If she were a good daughter, she would have given Aunt Lydia some of her money. Poor Aunt Lydia has gone through her trust fund like it would magically regenerate," Emerson said.

I bit my tongue not to jump in and ask if he tried to borrow money from Paige, too. Rob did it for me.

"Have you or your mother borrowed money from Paige? If so, is it documented?" Rob said.

"No, we did not. We didn't need Paige's money. My mother and I are fine." Emerson's voice didn't sound so certain, though.

"Thank you for your time, Mr. Merritt. We will be in touch as soon as we have more information." Christine reached out to shake Emerson's hand. He shook it with no effort and did the same to Rob.

He raced away from the detectives and pulled his mother out of a conversation. They scuttled back into the main house, acknowledging no one on their way.

In contrast, Rob and Christine acknowledged me.

"I assume you overheard all that, Sammy." Christine stood next to at the courtyard wall. "And don't tell me you have an interest in botany."

"Yes, and you're right, I don't care about ivy," I said. "But since you're here, I can tell y'all about my conversation with Winston last night."

"We've talked to him already, but let's hear what he told you," Rob said.

After I finished, Rob said, "Yes, that's what he told us. Seems like he's being honest."

"He said he was scared and wanted police protection. Did he name the person who he's frightened of?" I said.

"Tate's killer. But we haven't officially confirmed it's a homicide," Christine said. "Winston has a flair for the dramatic. But if we thought he was in danger, he would have protection."

"That makes sense. You haven't gotten Hollis's autopsy report back yet, have you?" I said.

"Not yet," Rob said."I think we've worn out our welcome, Christine. We should go now."

"Before you go, I need to tell you that Frank Fortuna will be calling you," I said.

"Frank the grandson? Not Frankie?" Christine asked.

"Correct. He has information about Emerson buying beer, the nonalcoholic kind," I said.

Christine stared at me with a puzzled look on her face. "Why does that matter?"

"According to Frank, he doesn't normally buy that kind of beer, but he did on the day Tate died."

"Frank is sure about this?" Rob said.

"He said he would look it up on the family's account. And I did tell him to call you," I said.

"He did leave me a voicemail, but I hadn't listened to it yet," Christine admitted.

"We can call him when we leave." Rob started to go, but Christine stopped him.

"Wait, a text came in from the coroner's office." Christine read the message and looked up at me. "You're not going to leave, are you?"

"No unless you really need me to." I smiled widely, hoping my charm would work on Christine.

"Yes, your smile is nice, but that doesn't work on me." Christine rolled her eyes.

"Go ahead and tell us both." Rob looked anxious.

"Tate had sleeping pills in his system along with the nonalcoholic beer. He didn't have a prescription for the medicine," Christine said.

"Interesting. Keep this to yourself, Sammy." Rob locked eyes with me.

Rob and Christine left and headed toward the courtyard gate. Dorothy followed them. Whether it was out of politeness, to scold them, or to make sure they actually left, I wasn't certain. Dorothy had a smile plastered on her face that gave little away.

Whoever killed Tate was reckless and stupid. Between all the true crime documentaries and podcasts, he or she must have known the police would run tests. To me, Tate's murder seemed to be done out of desperation.

I joined Aunt Charlene and Nora by the water fountain. Chills ran down my spine as I recalled finding Paige here. I didn't blame Lydia for hiding inside. A podium stood in front of the fountain, with all the chairs facing it.

Nora leaned out of her wheelchair and placed her hand on the bricks surrounding the water basin. "Did you find Paige here, Sammy?"

"Yes, I did," I said.

"I'm not a psychic or medium, but I feel Paige's spirit here," Nora said.

"We should have brought Ruby," Aunt Charlene said.

"Ruby, is that your next door neighbor, right Sammy? She saw spirits around me that night in your courtyard." Nora perked up.

"I think Paige is here, too." Lydia suddenly appeared next to us. She looked like a ghost with her pale skin and red-ringed eyes.

"Lydia, I'm so glad to see you." Nora reached for Lydia's hand and held it.

"I'm happy you're here. Again, I'm so sorry about my outburst the other night." Lydia pulled a chair close to Nora and sat down.

"I understand. We all understand. You've lost so much, Lydia," Nora said.

"So have you." Lydia turned to Momo. "Also, you, Momo."

"Yes, we have. Despite everything, we're here, living life to the fullest," Momo declared.

"Amen," my aunt said.

"Do you feel Hollis out here, too?" Nora asked Lydia.

"Oh, yes. Both Paige and Hollis passed away in this spot." Lydia rubbed the bricks where we had found Paige. "After Hollis died, I wanted the fountain drained. But Dorothy overruled me."

Confusion crossed Nora's face. "I thought Hollis died over there."

Nora pointed across the courtyard. "He was lying on the ground in the middle, over there. I didn't know they found him in the fountain."

"You didn't?" Lydia tilted her head in confusion. "Oh, you left before we received the final autopsy report. Hollis drowned."

29

───────

"He drowned?" Nora croaked. "I thought he died from hitting his head on the ground. That's where he was when I left that night."

"See, you had nothing to do with Hollis's death. He drowned in the fountain after falling face-first into the bricks," Lydia explained. "I know you always thought that you were partly responsible for Hollis's death, but you weren't. He most likely was drunk and stumbled into the fountain."

Both Nora and I were shocked. Nora told me that Hollis was alive when she left and nowhere near the fountain. She believed he died from hitting the back of his head on the ground. No one mentioned drowning.

"Lydia, I hate to ask this, but did Hollis hit the back or the front of his head?" I said.

She squeezed her eyes shut, and I regretted asking her. It seemed heartless to make her face such a painful memory. Asking that at her daughter's memorial service felt wrong. My stomach hardened at my callousness.

Lydia didn't take offense, to my amazement. Her eyes

fluttered open. "He had a wound across his forehead and bruises around his shoulders. Our mother demanded an open casket, so the mortician worked all night."

"You didn't know, Nora?" Lydia said. "Oh, you left right after the funeral, and we didn't get the autopsy report until weeks later. And the family didn't talk about it. We just said he died from an accident. It was uncouth to go into details according to Dorothy."

"You're saying Hollis drowned in the water fountain?" Nora's voice shook.

"Yes, I remember the report said there was blood on the bricks around the fountain. He must have hit his head there and fallen in the water. It seems as if the fall knocked him unconscious and he couldn't get himself up." Tears streamed down Lydia's face. "This fountain is cursed. This house is cursed. This family is cursed."

Momo enveloped Lydia in a hug and let her cry. The grief from Lydia and Nora was palpable. They both needed this release, I believed. Dorothy didn't feel the same.

"Lydia, control yourself. This isn't the time or the place," Dorothy stomped over to rebuke her sister.

"This is a memorial. People are supposed to grieve here, Dorothy!" Momo's anger and frustration made her seem ten feet taller.

Dorothy took a step back and gawked at Momo. I swore I could see the gears turning in her head. Would she agree with Momo or argue with her? All eyes were on her.

"Yes, of course." Dorothy rubbed her temples with her hands. "We're all grieving in our own way. Let me have Emerson take you inside for a bit, Lydia. We'll start the service in ten minutes."

Dorothy kissed her sister on the cheek and headed toward Emerson.

"She means well, she really does." Lydia took the tissue I offered her and wiped her face. "I haven't slept well for days."

"No one expects you to be at your best," Aunt Charlene said.

"Lack of sleep affects me deeply." Lydia stood up and wobbled for a second, but caught her balance. "I misplaced my sleeping pills and haven't replaced them yet."

Emerson joined us with a sour look on his face. "Momma said to take you inside to rest, Aunt Lydia. I can make you a cup of tea, too."

"Thank you, Emerson." She accepted his outstretched arm and leaned on him. "And thank you to all of you ladies for listening to me. Paige loved you so much, Nora and Momo."

Her nephew led away Lydia. Once they were gone, I took Lydia's seat next to Nora.

"See, Nora, you didn't kill Hollis. He must have fallen onto the fountain, hit his head, and then slipped into the water," I explained.

"Paige seemed surprised I had never heard the results of the autopsy. She said I was wrong, and I had nothing to do with Hollis's death," Nora said.

"Did she tell you about the drowning?" I said.

"No." Nora emphatically shook her head. "Paige said I must not have all the details. She promised to get the complete story for me. Is that the reason she was murdered?"

I grasped Nora's hands. "We don't know just yet. But we are going to find out. I promise."

Nora squeezed my hands before we moved to the back to take our places for the memorial service. I tried to focus on the speeches from Paige's friends and family, but I couldn't.

My mind was spinning from all this information. Why did the family hide how Hollis died if it was an accidental drowning? Was there something on the autopsy report that disputed Hollis's manner of death?

I had more questions for Nora after the service. Seeing the grief in her eyes made me more determined to get answers about Hollis's and Paige's deaths for her.

30

———

"Sammy, join me in my bedroom. We need to talk." Nora climbed up the steps to Momo's house with Aunt Charlene's help after the memorial.

"Do we want tea or bourbon?" Momo asked as the door shut behind us.

"Bourbon," we all said at once.

"And this is why I like you people." Momo went directly to the kitchen to get our drinks.

"Sammy, can you help Nora to her room?" Aunt Charlene said. "I'll help Momo."

We entered her bedroom and found Lady Clementine lying on the bed. She perked up when Nora climbed under the covers.

"Hello, my pretty kitty." Nora stroked Lady Clementine's soft fur. "Siamese kitties are so pretty."

"I agree, but don't let my cat hear that." I took a seat on the edge of the bed. "Are you feeling up to talking?"

"Yes. I feel like we've found all these puzzle pieces, but now how do they go together?"

"That's a perfect way to describe it." I sighed. "So let me

tell you what I think has happened. First, let's start with Hollis's death."

Nora settled into her bed, her back resting on the headboard. Lady Clementine curled up next to her. And I began with my theories.

"First, I don't think you killed Hollis. Lydia told us he had moved from where you left him. Why did they hide the drowning from you? From everyone? Remind me who was at the house that night."

Nora drew in a long breath. "Their parents were out of town, but Dorothy and Lydia were there. Paige, the baby, was in the main house. Emerson would have been home, too. His metal race cars were all over the courtyard as usual."

"You told me on Thanksgiving that Hollis was annoyed with Emerson and his cars. Is it possible that he tripped on them? Maybe that's why he fell into the fountain," I said.

"It's possible. Especially since he was drunk. He would have been furious with Emerson if that had happened. Once, I saw Hollis throw Emerson's cars in the fountain to keep him away from us."

"I agree." I tapped my feet in frustration. All I had were ifs and possibilities. "Would there be another reason he'd be by the fountain or even in it?"

Nora's eyes lit up. She opened the nightstand and took out Hollis's card. "He was supposed to have another gift for me. Read the poem."

I read out loud: "It's tucked away safely, hidden from view. A surprise from me, just waiting for you."

"Hollis and his sisters had a secret spot behind the water fountain. He showed me once. You have to step into the fountain to get to it. I don't quite remember which brick you had to pull out to find the hiding place," Nora said.

"That could be the reason he was in the fountain, then. But how did he get a wound on his forehead?"

"He could have spun around after he took out whatever he hid and then fell," Nora said.

"True. But I'm still hung up on why the family hid the fact he drowned."

Nora's eyes drifted shut, and she jerked herself awake. "Sorry, I didn't realize how exhausted I was."

Nora's energy drained like a battery in a noisy kid's toy. "You should rest, Nora. It looks like Lady Clementine is ready to settle down with you."

The cat was curled up right against her with her paws over Nora's legs. Lady Clementine's eyes and body language radiated seriousness and firmness. She appeared to be protecting Nora.

"I will, but I have a huge favor to ask." Nora opened her eyes. "I would really like to know what Hollis hid for me. If Lydia is home, she'll let you in the courtyard. You can tell her what you're looking for."

"If she's not available, should I ask Dorothy or Emerson?" I headed to the bedroom door.

"If you think you can trust them, yes. But Sammy, please be careful. I can't lose someone else before I go." Nora settled back into the bed with her guardian cat.

I would be careful, but I was determined to find Hollis's gift for Nora. She needed it. She also needed to know the truth about what happened to Hollis and Paige. The answers had to be at the Davenport home.

31

I prayed as I made my way back to the Davenport House. Please let Lydia open the door. I trusted her more than her sister and nephew. If Lydia didn't open the door, I hadn't figured out what I would say to them. I might risk asking them for access to the courtyard. Only Nora knew where I was going. I didn't tell Aunt Charlene and Momo since I was positive they would insist one of them should go with me. A one-on-one conversation seemed the best way to approach Lydia.

Lydia answered my prayers by opening the front door. She wore her black dress from the memorial, but her hair was falling out of its bun. "Samantha, what are you doing here? Is Nora okay?"

"Nora is fine—no, she isn't," I said. "She's exhausted, both mentally and physically. Nora asked me to do one thing for her."

"What is it?" Lydia's eyes grew larger, and she appeared more awake than she had during the service.

"Hollis left a riddle in that birthday card. We're pretty

sure we know where to find the other gift Hollis left. May I go to your courtyard?"

"Now? It's rather late." Lydia looked at her watch. "Oh, it's only seven. The day has been so long."

"I wouldn't have come to you if I didn't think Nora needed to find the gift."

Lydia studied my face. "Do you think Nora is going to die soon? If that's the case, let's go."

"Thank you so much, Mrs. Townsend."

"We'll go through the courtyard gate. Dorothy is napping on the couch, and we don't want to wake her." Lydia punched in a code to the courtyard gate and we entered.

The chairs and the podium were stacked in the back. The only sound was the trickling water from the fountain. I headed toward it and slipped off my shoes.

"What are you doing?" Lydia stared at me.

"Nora believes her gift is in the brick hiding place." I pointed to the ivy-covered wall.

"I haven't thought about that spot in years." There was a spark of life in her eyes. "Hollis would have used that to hide a gift. The hiding place is six bricks to the left of the water-spout and six bricks up. It should still be loose."

I stepped into the fountain basin one foot at a time. The chill of the water hurt my feet, but I had to ignore it. I counted the bricks as Lydia said and found a loose one. Carefully, I pulled it out and placed it on the edge of the fountain.

Lydia sat on the edge of the fountain with her eyes focused on the now empty spot. I reached into the opening, hoping a family of spiders hadn't taken residence inside. My fingers felt a metal object, and I pulled it slowly out.

"That looks like one of Emerson's cars," Lydia exclaimed.

I had found a tiny red metal race car. It couldn't have been Hollis's gift. While Lydia held the car, I reached into the hole once more. This time I brought out a flat white square box bound with a red ribbon.

"This must be it." I gripped the box in my hands so I wouldn't drop it. The gift, tucked away for years, finally emerged.

"Hollis must have tied that ribbon. He was always messy." Lydia smiled. "Are you going to open it?"

Although I was dying to see what was inside, I didn't open it. The gift was meant for Nora, and she deserved to see what was inside first. I put the box in my dress pocket. "No, I'll take it to Nora."

Lydia's shoulders drooped, but she kept smiling. "I'd like to go with you when you give it to Nora."

I stepped out of the fountain and shook the water off my feet. "Let me put my shoes back on and we'll go."

"Thank you so much. Any bit of Hollis makes me happy."

I would let Nora decide if she wanted anyone around when she opened the box. Lydia could come with me, as it would give me more time to talk to her. There was something about that piece of Hollis's autopsy report in Paige's hand which nagged at me. Why did someone want that autopsy report to stay hidden?

Just as I slipped my shoes on, angry voices startled me. Lydia and I turned around to find Emerson stomping out of the main house with his mother right behind him.

"I told you the autopsy report didn't show anything to worry about, Mama! If Paige had just given me the report, she'd be alive."

32

After Emerson's outburst, he and his mother noticed Lydia and me. The water fountain sounded like thunder in the awkward silence. Emerson and his mother stayed in their spots, about ten feet away from us. Lydia moved closer to me and held my hand.

"Lydia, I thought you were napping in your room," Dorothy said.

"I-I tried, but my sleeping pills are missing," she stammered.

"Did you take them, Emerson?" My insides felt like jelly, but I kept my voice even and calm. Having someone confess to murder was not a good situation to be in.

"Why would I do that?" Emerson tried to sound casual, but his face betrayed his fear.

"You must have used them to drug Tate King. He didn't have a prescription for the pills found with him. And you were seen buying nonalcoholic beer the day he died," I said. "I imagined Tate called to blackmail you. Killing him was easier, wasn't it?"

"Yes. I couldn't risk that Paige had told him about the

autopsy report. I just needed him out of our lives for good," Emerson said.

"You did that, too?" Dorothy grabbed her son's arms and shook him like a rag doll. "You didn't need to kill either of them. Hollis's autopsy report showed it was an accident. You didn't kill him."

"No, I didn't kill Hollis. But you did, Mom." Emerson's knees dropped to the ground. "I know you did it to protect me."

Lydia dropped my hand and strode over to her sister. "What are you talking about? Hollis was murdered? Which of you did it?"

"I have a theory." Once again, the three of them looked at me as if I had just shown up. "Hollis was angry after Nora left that night. Did you come down to get your cars and Hollis yelled at you? Did you two get into a fight?"

"We did. He always hated me." Emerson stood back up, his knees shaking. "I tried to ignore him and went to put my new car in the hiding spot in the wall. He tried to yank me away, but I put the car inside it and put the brick back."

"Did he take the rest of your cars? Nora said they were scattered around the courtyard," I said.

"He did. I yelled at him, but he wouldn't give them back. I pushed him into the fountain, and then I went upstairs to get mom. He was alive when I left him, I swear," Emerson said.

"See, Emerson had nothing to do with Hollis's death," Dorothy pleaded with her sister.

"Then why did he take the autopsy report from Paige?" Lydia snapped.

"Because Dorothy killed Hollis," I said. "You were protecting your son."

"You were there? The night Hollis died?" Lydia's face

turned purple. "You said you found him in the morning. What did you do?"

Dorothy sat on the edge of the fountain. She clutched Emerson's car in her hands. "I came to the courtyard and found Hollis splattering around like a fish. He was grumbling about Emerson, about being sick of his family obligations, and about me."

Dorothy warned Hollis that she would tell their parents about his drinking if he didn't change his behavior toward Emerson. He laughed and said it didn't matter because he was leaving with Nora.

"He told me he was sick and tired of the family trying to run his life. I lost it." Dorothy began sobbing. "He was supposed to love us the most. The Davenport business and home were his responsibility. I lashed out at him."

"By lashing out, you pushed him headfirst into the edge of the fountain," I said.

"Yes. I didn't mean to hurt him. I just needed him to stop talking and listen to me," Dorthy said in between taking deep breaths.

"I still don't understand why you just didn't tell me. It sounds like an accident." Lydia sat next to her sister but didn't touch her. "Did you leave him, and then he drowned?"

"Yes, that's it." Dorothy didn't sound convincing.

Lydia studied her sister, making even me uncomfortable with her deep stare. "You held him in the water. I remember he had bruises around his shoulders. You killed him."

"I had to! He would tell our parents and my husband what I did. My relationship with all of them was rocky. This would have just ruined any goodwill I had with them. My husband would have taken Emerson." Dorothy's chest heaved as she cried. "I love my brother, but I love my son more."

"So when Nora said she shouldn't have killed Hollis, Paige looked for the autopsy report," I said.

Emerson finally spoke up. "I ran into her in the courtyard while I was out here having a drink. She said she was going to take it to Nora, but she wanted to show it to her mom first. Paige thought Nora needed to know that she had nothing to do with Hollis's death."

"Paige had a big heart. Unlike you and your mother." Lydia's face grew red. "But why did you kill her? All she was going to do was show Nora the report."

"I couldn't take the risk she wouldn't start looking into Hollis's death. She'd be the one to notice the bruise marks in the report. Paige always said something seemed off about the story of that night," Emerson said.

"You killed my daughter on the possibility she would find out what really happened?" Lydia ran over to Emerson and pushed him, but he didn't move. "You are as cruel and selfish as your mother."

Dorothy protested she wasn't, and the three of them began shouting at each other. As their mutual rage grew, I realized I needed to get out of here and call Rob.

"Hey, where do you think you're going?" Emerson left his mother and aunt and grabbed my arm. He yanked me back toward them. "You can't leave and tell your police friends what we said."

"Emerson, you can't kill her." Dorothy pulled him away from me.

"Then what are we going to do?" Emerson shouted. "You might not go to jail for Uncle Hollis's death, but they'll get me for Paige's and Tate's murders."

Dorothy glared at me with such anger. "If you had just left us alone, Samantha, we wouldn't be in this predicament. My son means more to me than you."

Emerson started toward me again, but Lydia stepped in between us. "You'll have to kill me first. There has been enough bloodshed in this family—for this family. No more."

"Lydia, no. We have to protect our family," Dorothy whined.

"Like you protected my daughter? Our brother? I will never trust you again."

"Fine." Dorothy pushed Lydia aside. "Emerson, how should we do this? Do you still have the pills you stole from Lydia?"

Lydia grabbed the brick that was still lying on the edge of the fountain. Dorothy ran toward her, and Lydia threw the brick toward me. My hands ached as I grabbed it, but I gripped it fiercely.

"Give me that!" Emerson rushed at me. When he was close enough, I hit him on the side of the head with the brick. He looked stunned, but then he fell to the ground.

Dorothy dropped next to Emerson and cradled his head. I grabbed Lydia's hand and pulled her into the main house. She locked the French doors as I called the police.

"Are you all right, Lydia?" I asked when I finished my call.

"No, but I will be." She embraced me. "Thank you for protecting me."

"I should say that to you. You can throw very well."

"The years of practicing my tennis serve finally were useful."

"Yes, it was." I looked out the windows at Dorothy and Emerson sitting on the ground together. Emerson was conscious, which was a relief. I didn't want to kill him, just get him away from Lydia and me.

The mother and son stayed together until the police arrived and separated them. That's when I burst into tears.

33

"It's always déjà vu with you, Sammy." Christine shook her head as she came into the kitchen where Lydia and I sat. I made tea, but neither of us touched it. I just nodded in response. My exhaustion had taken over.

"You'll be fine." Christine took a seat in between us and put a hand on my back. "I can talk to Mrs. Townsend first. Can we do that?"

"Yes. I want the whole truth about what Emerson and Dorothy have done." Lydia must be tired, but she rallied as she explained everything that happened tonight. I added bits of information as she talked. Her courage gave me the energy to finish the story.

"I'm so sorry you endured this, Mrs. Townsend," Christine said after Lydia finished.

"I wouldn't have survived without Samantha's help." Lydia grabbed a tissue from the box on the table. "You and Paige could have been wonderful friends. I've never met another woman as brave and caring as my daughter."

"That describes Sammy." Christine smiled at me.

Christine could have added her own adjectives, but she

chose not to. I wasn't sure if they would be positive or negative attributes. But right now, I didn't care. All I wanted to do was get to Nora. I had so much information to share.

And a box to give her.

Despite the late hour, I insisted on delivering the box to Nora. Rob had a police officer walk me to Momo's house. He also let our group chat know I was fine. And he called Momo to let her know, too. Rob made sure my family and friends heard what had happened before it hit the news.

Aunt Charlene and Momo had blown up my phone with voicemails and text messages, so I knew they were still awake.

"Sammy, my sweet baby girl!" Aunt Charlene threw open the front door and barreled down the steps. For once, I welcomed her tight embrace and squeezed her back just as hard.

"I'm all right. Don't cry." I wiped my own tears away. "Everything is all right."

"Let me hug her, too." Momo wormed her way in between Aunt Charlene and me. "I'm so thankful you're okay."

"Poor Lydia isn't." A lump formed in my throat. "She's lost everyone."

"No, she hasn't." Momo squeezed my hands. "She has me."

"Me, too," Aunt Charlene said.

"And as long as Nora is alive, she'll be there for Lydia." Momo's eyes watered. "I've told Nora what happened, but she wants to hear it from you."

I followed Momo and Aunt Charlene into the house. I

went to Nora's bedroom while they went to the kitchen to get me a cup of tea with a splash of bourbon. The door was open, but I stopped in the doorway. I held in a gasp; Nora had taken a turn for the worse. Her face looked pale, her eyes glazed, and her breathing shallow. Lady Clementine meowed from her spot next to Nora.

"Nora? May I come in?" I stepped into the room.

"Yes, please sit." Nora patted the spot next to her on the bed. "As you've probably guessed, I'm on my way out."

"Don't say that, Nora." I sat next to her and grasped her stiff hand.

"Sammy, you know it's true. I'm coming to terms with it." She smiled weakly. "I'd be much more at ease if I had some answers before my death. I got the gist of the story from Momo, but I want to hear it from you."

For the next thirty minutes, I told Nora what happened at the Davenport House. She cried as I recounted how Dorothy and Emerson confessed to the murders. When I finished, we sat in silence. Her tears subsided as Lady Clementine snuggled closer to her.

"What a horrible ending to so many lives. I have the truth I needed, but it shattered a family," Nora said.

"They were already falling apart. This was not your fault. Hollis wanted to leave with you. You were his future." I took the gift box out of my pocket. "This is what he left for you."

Nora's hands shook as she grasped the box. "I can't believe it was still there."

I helped her with the ribbon and gave it to Lady Clementine. She didn't play with it like I expected; she wasn't leaving Nora's side.

Nora opened the lid and pulled out a bracelet. Two gold

bangles were linked, and a red heart charm dangled from one of them.

"I can't believe he bought this for me." Nora held the bracelet in her hands. "I saw it in a shop here in the Quarter, but it was too expensive. The next time I went into the store, it was gone and I was heartbroken."

I took the bracelet and put it on Nora's wrist. "It's time to let go of the past. You always had Hollis's heart, and here's the proof."

"Yes. Yes, I do." Nora cried as I gently held her. Tears rolled down my face, too. I was thankful I found the answers Nora needed. But now that she had the truth, I believed she would leave us sooner rather than later.

34

———

"**A**re you ready? Prepare yourself for the best birthday party of your life!" Connor led me into the courtyard of Thibodeaux Mansion. He took me to dinner at Napoleon House while Aunt Charlene and her cohorts set up the party.

Despite my exhaustion from Sunday's confrontation with Emerson and Dorothy, I was actually excited about the party. After so much tragedy, we all needed a fun night.

Momo and Aunt Charlene were taking turns sitting with Nora. She was in and out of consciousness, but she wasn't in any pain. I went by earlier in the day to see her, but she was asleep.

Rows and rows of string lights illuminated the courtyard, which was filled with clusters of yellow, green, and purple balloons. If it wasn't for the huge "Happy Birthday Sammy!" banner across the back courtyard wall, it would have looked like a Mardi Gras party.

The courtyard held tables, each decorated with a cat-safe yellow Gerber daisy arrangement. All kinds of foods, from mac 'n' cheese to jambalaya to mini muffuletta sandwiches, filled a large buffet table. As promised, Aunt Charlene kept with her double theme with two cakes. The first was a three tier red velvet cake and the other a mocha doberge cake.

Next to the food, a bartender offered soda, sweet tea, beer, wine, and cocktails. As I expected, Aunt Charlene and Rose had come up with two special drinks for the evening: a Satsuma Pimm's Cup and a Rose French 75.

"Happy Birthday!" shouted my friends and family.

"Hi!" I yelled above the noise.

Connor escorted me through the crowd to a dance floor set up in the back of the courtyard. A three-piece band was waiting to play, but first Connor took the microphone.

"Hey, everyone! Thanks for coming to Sammy's birthday party. We especially appreciate y'all coming on a weeknight. This was the only time everyone could get together."

"And no one wants to miss a party thrown by Aunt Charlene!" Neal shouted from the crowd.

"Tru dat! Come on up here, Aunt Charlene," Connor said.

Dressed in a shimmering pink dress with her hair teased to the heavens, Aunt Charlene took the microphone from Connor. "I'm so glad we could get together to celebrate our Samantha. Before my niece came back into my life, I always said blood was thicker than water. But now that I've met all you wonderful people, I understand why she calls you family."

A chorus of "Awww" came from the crowd.

"You're part of our family now, Charlene!" Libby yelled out.

"Thank you, darling! I'm so glad you said that because I'm staying in New Orleans permanently!" Aunt Charlene grinned from ear to ear. "Happy Birthday, Sammy!"

The crowd cheered, and the band played. Jasper came up to me and put his arm around me. "So, is this the birthday gift you envisioned?"

"She's going to live with Momo, isn't she?"

"Yep. They're good for each other," Jasper squeezed me tight. "And Terry will keep her busy, too."

Aunt Charlene and Terry were already dancing. This was the first time since I met him he wasn't wearing paint stained clothing. He wore stiff blue jeans and a maroon button-down shirt. His hands and hair were free of paint, too. They made a cute couple. "I think we'll be all right."

For the next few hours, I roamed around the courtyard. Mr. Hugo and I danced as I promised. Even Andrew agreed to dance with me, but he drew the line at learning Neal's choreography for a line dance. Frankie came with three lasagnas and my favorite chocolate chip cookies.

Sissy twirled around on the dance floor with Rob. They made such a lovely couple. It was a preview of them dancing at their wedding. Nubi, Cleopatra, and Nefertiti snuggled amongst the plants of the water fountain. Their heads constantly moved as they watched the dancers. I think Sissy was their favorite, but I bet they were also hoping she would offer them snacks.

The cats knew better than to hang out by the buffet table. I overheard Ruby giving them strict instructions not to jump on the tables of food. I could have sworn they nodded their heads, but that might have been the Satsuma Pimm's Cup going to my head.

Papa danced with Christine. Ruby looked on with one of her rare smiles. Maybe she'd dance later, Libby kept refilling her wineglass, so maybe she was hoping to see her dance, too. Andre, Beau, Rose, and Mr. Hugo were laughing non-stop at a table. Neal cut in to dance with Aunt Charlene.

Terry did begrudgingly in jest, but asked Neal not to take too long. The smile that crossed Aunt Charlene's face was beautiful.

While waiting, Terry came over to me. "Cher, why aren't you dancing? You don't have two left feet. I've seen you shake a leg to the bands on Royal Street."

"I'll get out there soon. I promise. It's fun to watch everyone enjoying themselves. Especially you and Aunt Charlene." I winked.

Terry blushed. "You don't mind me courting your aunt, do you? Jasper said it was OK, so I figured you would, too."

"It's fine with me, I promise." I hugged Terry.

"Thanks, cher." Terry smiled as bright as the lights in the courtyard. "I might as well get a drink while I wait."

"Finally, I get a chance to be with the birthday woman." Connor snuck up behind me and put his arms around my waist.

I spun around and stood on my tiptoes to kiss him. At this moment, all was right with the world. "Yes, it's time for us to dance."

"And I've got the perfect song." Connor went up to the band and then came back to me.

We headed to the dance floor. The next song was "At Last", one of my favorites.

"Did you pick this song because I love it or are you pointing out we're now just dancing?" I laughed as we swayed to the music.

"Both." Connor's smile melted my heart. "But also you're finally taking the time to enjoy yourself and not worrying about everyone else."

We continued to dance, but he was wrong about me not worrying. Nora and Momo were on my mind. I wished they both could have been here.

After a few songs, I insisted on a break. Aunt Charlene and Terry were sitting at the table by my apartment. She waved me over.

"Come sit down, honey. Terry is going to get us some more drinks," she said.

"I'll be right back, ladies." Terry offered me his seat, and he headed to the bar.

"Aunt Charlene, I can't thank you enough for the party. It's been wonderful."

"I'm so glad you like it." She reached across the table and grabbed my hands. "I need to tell you why I wanted the double theme. It wasn't just because you have two birthdays. I needed to make sure you knew we care about the life you had after the hurricane. Your adopted parents raised you with a new birthday, so I want to respect that. But I wanted to tell you we never forgot about your actual birthday or that we forgot about you."

"I know you didn't, Aunt Charlene." I could feel tears welling up. "But I don't need to celebrate two birthdays. I don't need two of everything to remember my birth family and my adopted parents. I'm grateful for all my family and friends. They mean the world to me."

"Hallelujah! I'm so happy to hear that." Aunt Charlene used a napkin to dry her eyes. "We're going to have so much fun with all this family now that I'll be here."

"We're all lucky to have you, especially Momo," I said.

Aunt Charlene and I went out to the dance floor with everyone else. Well, except Ruby. I guess she had her limits. As Connor twirled me around, I spotted Momo walking into the courtyard. I rushed over to her, but I knew what was on her mind.

"Nora passed away, didn't she?" I hugged Momo before she could answer.

"She did a few hours ago. Once she started talking to Hollis and her parents, I knew it was time." Momo sighed. "Before my husband died, he spoke to his deceased family, so I was prepared. Or at least I thought I was."

"I don't think you can ever be ready for that. Would you like to sit down? I'm sure we have bourbon at the bar." I gestured toward my table.

"I'd love that bourbon, but let me give you something first."

I recognized the box instantly. "Lady Clementine refused to give up the ribbon, but I didn't think you'd care. Nora wanted you to have this."

The tears flowed as I opened the box and took out the bracelet. I put it on, feeling the weight of the love attached to it. "I will treasure this always."

"I know you will, sweetheart." Momo wiped the tears from my face. "Now let's go get that bourbon and celebrate the life of Nora Winslow."

As I walked with Momo to the bar, my head felt dizzy. Not from copious amounts of sugar and drinks, but from the love that surrounded me. I took an enormous risk moving to New Orleans on my own. Having a family like this is something I never dreamed of.

This was my best birthday yet. Or rather birthdays. Being able to embrace my past with my present was a gift I now appreciated. Life in New Orleans was more than I could ever have imagined. And growing old here was just what I wanted.

Sammy's next adventures continue in A Courtyard Conundrum.

ACKNOWLEDGMENTS

As always, thank you to my husband and children for all their love, support, and ideas for my books. Y'all get me through the good and the bad times.

Thank you to Dipper and Mabel, the sweetest cats, who inspire my fictional cats. I promise I'll put you in a book soon.

Dad and Wanda, thank you for your encouragement always.

Thank you to all the wonderful writers who have become friends over the years. Whether we meet in person, text, or chat online, your encouragement and support is unbelievable.

Thank you to Heather and Emily for sharing your stories. Keep them coming. You never know where they'll show up in my books.

Thank you to my family, friends, and readers for being here for me and my books!

ABOUT THE AUTHOR

Jen Pitts is a lifelong mystery reader who turned her obsession into writing cozy mysteries of her own. When she isn't plotting fictional murder, she's chugging coffee, traveling to New Orleans, reading, and enjoying life with her husband, children, and two cats in the Pacific Northwest.

Learn more about Jen through her newsletter. A free short story prequel is available exclusively for newsletter members. Sign up at www.jenpittsauthor.com

And keep up daily with Jen on Facebook where she shares her books, her cats, and her love of New Orleans.

You can also find Jen on the following social media sites:

facebook.com/jenpittsmysteryauthor

instagram.com/jenpittsmysterywriter

goodreads.com/jenpitts

amazon.com/author/jenpitts

bookbub.com/authors/jen-pitts

ALSO BY JEN PITTS

The French Quarter Mystery Series:

Coffee, a Scone, and a Place to Call Home - a Short Story Prequel

The Key to Murder

The Gates to the Afterlife

A Deadly Check-In

Bury the Past

The Dead End Tour

A Corpse in the Cafe

Happy Homicide

The Witches of the French Quarter Series:

Mardi Gras and Magic

Red Beans and Rituals